The Dark Locket

SECRETS OF THE SANATORIUM

CHRIS WITT

Chris Witt

Table of Contents

❀ Created with Vellum

For Jeremiah,

My light in the darkest corridors,

and for those who dare to uncover the truth

hidden within the shadows.

May courage always guide your journey.

CHAPTER 1

The Disappearance

I tapped my finger against the rim of my fourth glass of wine; my gaze fixated on the clock as if staring could change the outcome. The second hand crawled, mocking me with its slow, deliberate tick. Eight o'clock. Impossible. Emily would never be three hours late. Of the two of us, I was the one constantly running behind. Emily was punctual, always waiting with that knowing smile and a spark of mischief in her eye.

"Harold," she'd tease, her voice laced with laughter, "do you make your patients wait this long, too?"

That was Emily—her blonde hair meticulously braided; her gray eyes distant until they found me. Every dinner, every study session, she'd be there first. Tonight was supposed to be different. I had made sure of that—dinner at my place; no chance of me being late this time. No excuses.

I glanced at the table set for two. The chicken croquettes lay cold and untouched, the gravy a congealed mess pooling beneath the breading. My eyes were drawn to the centerpiece—a small black box, unopened. Inside, a simple gold band awaited. Small, unassuming, yet perfect for her. I envisioned it on her hand—the way her eyes would light up when she saw it—the moment I'd been dreaming of for weeks.

The apartment was small but cozy, a combination of kitchen, entryway, and dining area all in one. A modest wooden table, scuffed but sturdy, occupied the center, surrounded by mismatched chairs that had seen better days. The kitchen was filled with the comforting scent of home-cooked meals, with pots and pans hanging above the stove.

On the opposite side of the apartment, a bedroom and bathroom provided a private retreat. Everything had its purpose—nothing overly ornate or extravagant, yet each piece seemed to hold a story of its own.

Like the ring. It wasn't expensive—far from it—but the simplicity felt right. It wasn't about the cost. It was about Emily, and I knew the moment she saw it, she'd understand.

The silence stretched on, thick and suffocating. My fingers twitched toward the rotary telephone on the side table, the urge to call gnawing at me. I'd already dialed her number twice, the dial spinning slowly beneath my fingertips. No answer. My stomach churned, tightening into knots. What if she hadn't heard it? Maybe she was deep into her dissertation, too absorbed in her work to notice the ringing.

Or maybe... she wasn't home at all.

"She's on her way," I muttered, though the words felt empty as if saying them could make it true. My voice barely cut through the stillness of the room.

Another glance at the clock. Three minutes had passed, but it felt like a lifetime. The scenarios ran wild in my head—had she tripped and twisted her ankle? Maybe she was lying in the street, helpless, trying to drag herself to safety. Or worse—hit by a car, broken and bleeding, calling out for me with her last breath. The image burned in my mind: Emily crumpled on the asphalt, her blonde hair matted with blood, a stranger kneeling beside her, holding her hand as she whispered my name.

A cold sweat broke out across my forehead, trickling down to my temples. I wiped it away with a shaky hand, but more beads of sweat quickly followed. My heart pounded, the thud echoed in my ears, and my throat was dry despite the wine. I downed the rest of it in one gulp, the glass clattering against the table. The sharp burn in my throat barely registered—just a brief flash of warmth, gone as quickly as it came.

I couldn't sit here spiraling any longer. My chest tightened with each passing second, my breathing ragged. The coat slipped from my hand as I fumbled for it, barely shoving my arms into the sleeves. My vision swam, my head light, and I stumbled toward the door, legs unsteady beneath me. My hand shook as I grabbed the knob, and I forced a deep breath, trying to pull myself together. But the panic gnawed at the edges of my thoughts, and the urge to *move* overwhelmed everything else.

Even though it was late, the oppressive heat of the night hit me like a wall as I stepped outside. The air was thick, clinging to my skin, and within seconds, my shirt was stuck to my back, damp with sweat. I fumbled with the knot of my tie, fingers shaking as I loosened it, but the fabric still felt like a noose around my neck.

By the time I reached Emily's townhouse, I was a mess. The cool, composed appearance I had left the apartment with was long gone —my black curls plastered to my forehead, my shirt sticking like a second skin, and the dampness spreading beneath my arms was unbearable. I barely noticed it, though. My focus was locked on her front door, looming ahead of me like a barrier between knowing and not knowing.

Taking a breath, I knocked—three sharp raps that seemed to echo far too loudly in the stillness of the night. The sound bounced off the quiet street, filling the silence, and I could feel my heart hammering in my chest, my breath shallow as I waited.

Nothing.

I knocked again, harder this time, the urgency creeping into my movements. I pressed my ear against the door, straining to hear anything—a creak, footsteps, her voice. But there was only silence, thick and impenetrable.

An older man in a long red robe appeared on the neighboring porch, his silhouette sharp under the dim porch light. He was glaring at me; his brows knitted together in clear irritation.

"Can I help you?" His voice cut through the night, a hint of condescension in his tone.

"E-Emily," I stammered, my tongue thick and sluggish from the wine. My thoughts were swimming, but I forced myself to focus. "She's not answering."

The man raised an eyebrow, clearly unimpressed. "Who?"

"Emily. The woman who lives here. Emily," I repeated, the desperation slipping into my voice.

"Right. Well—" His arms folded were tightly across his chest, his stance stiff and unyielding. "Why don't you go home and try calling her tomorrow? When you're a little more... presentable."

His words stung, but I pushed past the fog in my mind. "No. You don't understand. I need to see her. I *need to*—" My throat tightened as the fear bubbled up again. I swallowed hard, forcing the rest of the sentence down. If I voiced my worry out loud, the spiral would start all over again. "Have you seen her?" I inquired, my voice dropping to a faint whisper.

The man's expression didn't soften. "Go home, son. If she's ignoring you, she has a good reason for it."

His words hit me like a slap, and I watched in silence as he turned on his heel, his robe swishing behind him as he disappeared back into his house. The door closed with a soft click, leaving me standing alone on the porch, his dismissal echoing in my head. Had I upset Emily? Was that why she wasn't answering?

Feeling the weight of everything crashing down, I sank onto the front step, my elbows on my knees, head in my hands. My mind raced back to the last time I'd seen her—two days ago. What had I missed? What had I said? I replayed every conversation, every glance, trying to find something, anything, that would explain why she wasn't here.

As I sat there, the memories flooded back, vivid and clear. We sat at Emily's favorite table at The Fig, a cozy café nestled in the heart of town. The air was thick with the aroma of fresh coffee and baked goods, but my mind was elsewhere. Papers lay strewn across the table like scattered thoughts, but Emily was engrossed in her tattered green journal. The book was worn and stained, its spine barely holding together, yet she clung to it fiercely, believing it contained the essence of her most important work—her dissertation. Even as its pages dwindled, she had ingeniously added more, refusing to part with it.

"Most people aren't interested in the Lyaeus sanatorium," she said, her brow furrowed in concentration. "Yet, if we simply overlook the past—"

"How can we ever be free of it?" I interjected, my curiosity piqued.

"Exactly! What kind of scholar would be deterred by a few ghost stories?"

"Maybe the concern isn't primarily with the ghosts but rather with the building itself." I picked up one of the images on the table—a striking portrayal of the sanatorium in its current condition. Though it had been only twenty years since its closure, the windows were boarded up, and the stone walls were shrouded in thick ivy, giving the place an air of decay and foreboding. "There's an unsettling quality about it."

Emily laughed softly. "Wrong? I didn't know we judged buildings by a moral compass."

"Not morally wrong. It's like... our minds pick up on subtle details without us realizing it. There's probably something about the design that just feels unsafe, which leads to the rumors."

She nodded thoughtfully. "And that's what causes people to think it's haunted. But if it were going to collapse, surely it would have by now."

"Not necessarily. It could still fall apart." I glanced back at the photo, unease creeping in. "Is it still possible to change your topic? Maybe focus on a different sanatorium."

"You're starting to sound like my advisor, Harold. Nothing is going to happen to me—at least not because of the building or—" She paused, shaking her head as if to dispel the thought.

"Hey—" I reached across the table, taking her hand and feeling the warmth of her skin. "I didn't mean to discourage you. If this is what you want to write about, then go for it. And if your advisor has a problem, show them a proposal so compelling they can't refuse."

She hummed softly, a mixture of hope and hesitation in her voice. "Could you help me with it?"

"I can give you some guidance, but I'm not certain how much it will assist you. My advisor was much easier to deal with. Plus, conducting experiments and writing about them is a whole different ball game."

Emily bit her lip, a flicker of frustration in her eyes. "You're right. It was naïve of me to bring it up."

"No, Emily—"

"I've just been feeling overwhelmed lately. It's like there are eyes on me, watching my every move."

"I understand. I felt that way last year, too. But even if you make a mistake—"

"No. It's not like that, never mind. You're right. I'm just stressed. I need something to look forward to."

As she spoke, the weight of the ring in my pocket felt heavier, a reminder of what I had planned. But this moment didn't feel romantic enough. She deserved something better. "How about I cook dinner for you at my place in a couple of days?"

A throat cleared nearby, pulling me out of my spiraling thoughts. I looked up to see a police officer standing on the sidewalk, his hand resting on his belt. His face was lined with experience, but his eyes held a calm authority. The name "Kantos" was stitched on his uniform.

I scrambled to my feet, my legs stiff from sitting for what felt like hours, replaying every detail repeatedly in my head.

"Evening," Kantos said, his voice calm but curious. "Everything alright?"

"I need to report a missing person," I blurted out, the words escaping before I could stop them.

His brow furrowed slightly as he stepped forward. "Who's missing?"

"My girlfriend, Emily. She lives here," I said, motioning toward the house. "We had plans to meet for dinner, but she never turned up. I've been calling her all night. I came here, but... she's not answering, and the house is dark. This isn't like her."

Kantos gave a brief nod, glancing at the house before turning back to me. "How long has she been missing?"

"Since this evening," I said, the tension in my voice was unmistakable. "But I know something's wrong. She wouldn't just disappear like this."

Before Kantos could say anything, another officer approached from the street. A tall, broad man with a red beard and an impatient expression, his uniform read "Benten." A prominent red scar ran down his left cheek.

"What's happening here?" Benten asked, giving me a wary look before shifting his gaze to the house.

Kantos nodded toward me. "He's reporting his girlfriend missing. Says she lives here."

Benten looked at me skeptically. "You sure she didn't just step out for the night? Maybe with a friend?"

I shook my head. "No, she wouldn't do that. I've been calling her for hours. I even checked with the neighbors. No one's seen her."

Benten grunted, unimpressed.

Kantos studied me for a moment, then asked, "Did she mention going anywhere? Any trips or plans?"

I opened my mouth to respond but stopped as a thought flashed through my mind—the sanatorium. Emily had been knee-deep in her dissertation research lately, spending a lot of time investigating that old, abandoned place. It wasn't far from town, but it was isolated and eerie. The idea sent a chill running down my spine. Could she have gone there?

"No, she didn't mention anything about leaving," I finally said, keeping my voice steady. "But this isn't normal. Something's off."

Kantos scribbled in his notebook, then looked at his partner. "We'll file a report, but unless there's any sign of foul play, there's not much more we can do tonight. If she doesn't show up by morning, give us a call."

I nodded, the words barely registering. My mind was already elsewhere, locked on the image of the sanatorium. I needed to go. I had to find out if she'd gone there.

Benten gave me a hard look. "Look, she's probably just out with a friend, or maybe she needed some space."

I didn't argue. I just needed them to leave.

Kanto glanced back at me with a sympathetic expression. "Go home. Try to get some rest. If anything changes or she still hasn't shown by tomorrow, we'll follow up."

I gave them a stiff nod, watching as they turned back toward their patrol car. The moment they were gone, I wasted no time. I headed straight home, my heart pounding as the sanatorium's shadow loomed larger in my mind.

CHAPTER 2

The Sanatorium Beckons

I t had taken me most of the night to unearth any information about the old Lyaeus Sanatorium

from dusty newspapers and a tattered book I'd found at a local bookshop. The flickering light from the lamp on my desk cast eerie shadows on the walls as I pored over pages filled with unsettling accounts and long-forgotten histories. When I finally stumbled upon the address, a strange sense of familiarity washed over me as if I had encountered it before but couldn't quite recall when or why. By the time I gathered enough details, dawn was breaking outside, yet the shadows still clung to the world.

As I drove toward the sanatorium, an unsettling sense of dread settled over me. The sunlight struggled to penetrate the thick canopy of trees lining the road, casting shadows that seemed to cling to the asphalt. The towering pines on either side reached out like gnarled fingers, their overgrown branches stretching ominously over the path.

Every instinct screamed at me to turn back. I rationalized that there were countless other places Emily could be, but the officers' words haunted me. I couldn't ignore the pull; something inside urged me onward.

As the trees thinned, the sanatorium rose ahead, a monstrous silhouette against the morning sky. It was a sight I recognized from the photos, yet it felt far more haunting in reality. The building loomed with an unsettling charm; an allure twisted by its history.

The first floor was a dark and imposing rectangle, its once-inviting entrance now obscured by a garden overtaken by wild ivy. The dense vines snaked up the stone walls, shrouding most windows in a dark embrace. A chill coursed through me, the garden a haunting reminder of what this place had once been—a threshold to a forgotten era.

The upper floors loomed above, each smaller than the one below, defying any sense of symmetry. Three circular towers protruded from the main structure: two nestled in the back corners and one standing ominously at the center. The second floor seemed to take on a life of its own, with walls forming a jarring U-shape that connected the central tower to the rest of the building, creating a triangle at its core. The unsettling architecture exuded a palpable sense of dread as if it were waiting, watching from the shadows.

Less ivy covered the upper levels, allowing glimpses of the windows, most of which were boarded up, yet the larger windows of the second floor remained intact, their glass gleaming menacingly in the morning light.

So engrossed was I in the haunting beauty of the sanatorium that I didn't notice the remnants of a rusted metal fence until it was too late. The car jolted violently, and I was thrown forward, my forehead nearly hitting the steering wheel.

"*Fuck!*" I cursed under my breath as I pushed the door open and stumbled out to evaluate the damage. The bumper was crumpled and bent inward; the left headlight shattered. "Just great."

Frustration bubbled up as I slammed my fist against the roof of the car, but I shook it off and refocused. If Emily was here, her car should be too. I scanned the area, my heart racing as I spotted a sleek black van parked at the edge of the garden. The van boasted a glossy finish, its sharp lines and modern design starkly contrasting with the dilapidated surroundings. With large, rounded headlights and a chrome grille, it exuded an air of unsettling sophistication, making it feel out of place amid the crumbling remnants of the sanatorium.

The part of me that wanted to flee screamed louder now, yet something compelled me to move closer to the van. My pulse quickened as I peeked through the tinted windows. On the passenger seat lay a familiar green, beat-up journal.

A whirlwind of thoughts surged through my mind. Why was the car here? Was Emily with its owner? Were they inside? But if they were, why hadn't she taken the notebook with her? My stomach twisted at the implications—she had mentioned feeling watched. I had brushed it off as paranoia, but what if it was real? What if someone had been following her?

I buried my head in my hands, forcing myself to breathe deeply. Panicking wouldn't do me any good. Once my legs steadied, I approached the front door. The once-vibrant red paint was nearly stripped away, exposing the pale wood beneath. An odd pattern was carved into the surface, its meaning lost in time. But what drew my eye was the absence of a doorknob—just an empty hole where it must have once been. I shoved against the door, but it resisted.

As I pondered whether to break it down, laughter drifted from the side of the building. For a fleeting moment, I thought it was Emily's, but the more I listened, the more I realized it was too light, too care-free—it was the laugh of a child.

I turned the corner, only to find the space deserted. "Is anyone there?" I called out, the word echoing in the oppressive silence.

Another laugh, deeper than the first, floated down from above. I looked up in time to see a pair of shoeless feet vanish into an open window on the second floor, the ivy below rustling as if in response.

"Hello?" I tried again, but I was more uncertain this time. "Kid?"

"Just start climbing, Harold!" The voice rang out, unmistakably the same one I had heard earlier—playful and oddly familiar.

Without thinking, I grabbed the wall, using the ivy to hoist myself up. Only as I pulled myself through the window did I realize the recklessness of my actions. I let out a nervous laugh, leaning against the wall as I tried to calm my racing heart. I felt foolish—one wrong move and I could have tumbled down, injuring myself. And why did that kid know my name? Did they know Emily? Had she mentioned me?

I bit my lip, forcing myself to scan the room. The child was nowhere to be found, which might have been for the best. The only furniture was a small, rusted metal bed frame pushed against one of the beige walls, seemingly dragged there to clear space for the unsettling drawings that covered the floor.

At the center of it all lay a dark crimson circular stain that stood out starkly against the faded beige wooden floor. The uneven strokes hinted at a chaotic hand, and I could make out several small handprints marred within the unsettling design. The longer I stared, the more I discerned the vague outline of a large feline in the center, surrounded by bizarre symbols that curled ominously around the edges. A gut feeling told me that this was blood.

I stood up and moved toward the door, carefully avoiding the ghastly circle, only to find the hallway was worse. A sickly blend of mold and a pungent, unrecognizable odor assaulted my senses, sending a chill down my spine. The faint light spilling from behind me revealed more of those strange symbols scrawled across the walls. While the floor was free of further drawings, it was littered with shards of glass and discarded needles.

For a fleeting moment, I wondered if this place had been a drug den or a haven for the homeless, but the unsettling stillness and absence of any signs of life told me otherwise. There was no evidence of food or drink, and the air was too stagnant, suggesting that no one had ventured into this part of the sanatorium for quite some time.

Yet, despite the fear coiling in my stomach, a peculiar sensation nagged at me—a strange sense of familiarity that was both unsettling and oddly comforting, as if the very walls recognized me. I shook off the thought, trying to clear it from my mind.

I caught my breath when an elusive image flickered in my mind. A chill swept through me, emanating from the building's depths. I briefly glimpsed something unsettling: a face, twisted and tormented. The moment I tried to focus on it, the image disappeared.

Then another sound emerged, echoing softly through the halls—a muffled cry that felt almost like a plea. It weighed heavily in my chest, leaving an unsettling feeling that lingered long after the sound faded away. The memory hung in the air, just beyond my reach, as if it were teasing me with its presence.

Before I could call out for Emily or the child I'd seen, something shifted at the end of the corridor. It was too dim to make out any details, but it resembled an older man. He crouched near one of the last doors before turning toward the spiral staircase nestled in the corner. Just as I thought I might get a better look; he vanished into the shadows.

A knot tightened in my stomach as Emily's words echoed in my mind—people believed this place was haunted. It felt foolish to entertain such thoughts, but…

I bit my lip, forcing myself to shake off the rising dread. "This place is playing tricks on you, Harold. Just find Emily."

I glanced at the stairs, momentarily considering pursuing the figure, but the thought made my chest constrict with anxiety. Instead, I resolved to explore the doors lining the hallway.

Each room mirrored the first: small and tainted with the same ominous red markings. Most had only empty bed frames, but a few were cluttered with disheveled mattresses strewn with empty bottles and dirty needles. Yet none revealed any trace of Emily, the child, or an escape route to avoid digging deeper into this oppressive place.

By the time I reached the end of the hall, my eyes had adjusted to the dim light, revealing more details. The staircase I had seen the figure on spiraled down to the first floor, and two more hallways branched off: one to the right and another leading diagonally down toward what must have been the central tower.

Just as I prepared to decide my next move, a piercing scream echoed from below. My heart plummeted as recognition struck me.

That was Emily.

I dashed down the staircase, urgency propelling me forward. Unlike the other rooms, the first floor was expansive and devoid of any bizarre symbols. Circular tables filled the space—each cluttered with books, cards, and board games—while worn armchairs encircled the room. Directly across from me stood another spiral staircase, and large double doors adorned with gold plaques lined the walls, save for the left side, which featured two smaller doors.

I blinked in surprise; at some point, the lights had flickered to life.

My attention snapped to the two doors as another scream pierced the air.

"Emily!"

"H-Harold?"

A breathless laugh escaped me; she was alive.

"I'm here! Just..." I glanced between the doors. "Keep talking!"

"Harold. Harold, please. Help me."

My gaze landed on the far door, marked as the Head Doctor's Office. I gripped the handle, only to find it stubbornly locked. "Damn it. Okay, Emily, stand back!"

"Harold. Please!"

I steadied myself before delivering a swift kick to the doorknob. Pain shot through my leg to my knee, but the door remained steadfast. I tried again and again, swallowing my curses with each failed attempt until the wood finally splintered under the force. With a final surge of determination, I shouldered the door.

As I stumbled into the room, light filtered through the gaps in the boards hastily nailed over the windows, illuminating the imposing desk in the center, the filing cabinets lining one wall, and, chillingly, the absence of another person in the room.

CHAPTER 3

Unraveling the Past

My voice wavered as I called out again, "Emily?"

I circled the room for the third time, convinced there had to be a hidden door or something I'd overlooked. I was sure I'd heard her voice from inside here—it didn't make sense she wasn't. Frustration gnawed at me as I started to make another round behind the desk, but my leg caught on something. One of the bottom drawers had been left open. I almost slammed it shut, annoyed with myself, until I saw what was inside.

The top of the file was caked in dust, but that didn't obscure the photograph clipped to it. Blonde hair neatly braided into a bun, gray eyes staring out, almost disinterested. She looked younger, her face softer with traces of baby fat still clinging to her cheeks, but it was unmistakably Emily.

My hands trembled as I lifted the file and placed it on the desk, staring at the label on the tab:

Emily Winters PN0003021943-03101943.

I froze. She hadn't mentioned ever being a patient here.

Flipping the file open, I expected pages of medical notes, treatment schedules, something. But instead, there was only a single sheet of paper filled with cryptic letters and numbers:

S1: 04.07.1945 - IC01

S2: 04.10.1945 - IC01

S3: 08.17.1948 - EW01

S4: 08.20.1948 - EW01

S5-003.12.1949 - EEW01

S6-003.30.1949 - EEW01

I traced the numbers with my finger. They felt oddly familiar. "Dates?" I muttered.

I scanned the room, my gaze landing on a metal filing cabinet tucked in the corner. I yanked the top drawer open, revealing a row of neatly stacked circular tapes. Pulling one out, I saw it was labeled with two codes—one that matched the patient number format next to Emily's name and another resembling the dates on the paper.

Heart pounding, I shoved the tape back and quickly rifled through the remaining shelves, each filled with tapes sorted by patient numbers. They were all organized in meticulous order. I just needed to find one linked to Emily, and I'd have all her recordings.

But halfway through my frantic search, I stopped. Emily was somewhere in this building, maybe in danger, and here I was, digging into her past, prying into something she might not even remember. She'd never mentioned being treated here, but there could be reasons for that. Fear, denial or maybe she simply didn't remember. If those dates were real, she would've been a child—just five during the last entry. Could I blame her if she blocked it out?

Shaking my head, I closed the drawer. I needed to find her, not her secrets.

I shoved the cabinets shut and forced myself to take a harder look at the room. I *knew* I'd heard Emily in here. If I wasn't ready to start believing in ghost stories, that meant there had to be something I was missing. Her voice had been level with mine, which meant she wasn't trapped below or calling from another floor. The left wall was shared with the adjacent room, so it couldn't be that one. That left the back and right walls.

I moved to the windows, peering through the narrow gaps between the planks. As expected, ivy had wound its way over the glass, but there was just enough space for me to glimpse the overgrown patch of grass beyond, leading to the thick line of pines—nothing new there.

That left the right wall.

At first glance, it looked no different from the others. The faded beige paint was smooth, with no cracks or damage, and the cobwebs were just as dense on this side as anywhere else. Still, something tugged at my instincts, urging me to check.

I pressed my hand against the wall, wincing as a puff of dust burst up from the surface, leaving a trail of grime in its wake. My fingers crept slowly across the surface, feeling for something—anything. About halfway across, I noticed the wall was warm in one spot, almost unnaturally so. I shifted my hand, and it dipped slightly as if there was a hidden indentation.

I frowned, running my hand back and forth. There—just below my thumb, something jutted out. I couldn't see it, but I could *feel* it beneath my fingertips. I squinted, trying to catch it from another angle, but the wall stayed stubbornly flat. Still, the indent was wider than me, and as I continued to feel around, my hand suddenly smacked into something cold and round.

A doorknob.

I hesitated only a moment before twisting it, and the wall swung inward, revealing a hidden room.

Unlike the rest of the sanatorium, which felt frozen in neglect and decay, this room looked lived-in. Cozy, even. The walls were painted a soft, warm orange, and a plush white rug covered the floor. In the center of the room was a bed draped in thick blankets and pillows that looked like they'd just been fluffed. A large dresser stood on the right wall, and the entire left wall was lined with mismatched book-shelves.

Curiosity tugged me toward the shelves. They were filled with a mix of fantasy novels, trinkets, and photographs. There were postcards from different places around the world, each carefully arranged to face the bed. Tiny figurines of animals stood like sentinels between the books. And then there were the photos—group shots, mostly of large groups of 30 people in various locations, some of them vacation spots, others outside the sanatorium itself.

But the last photo made my stomach twist. It was newer than the others, and there was only one person in it—Emily. She was smiling, her blonde hair pulled back in a neat braid, and she was wearing the shirt I knew she saved for special occasions.

I knew this photo.

I had been there the day it was taken, her final day of classes. I'd surprised her with lunch, and she'd waved at me just as the photographer snapped the picture. I remembered how she'd been scolded for not taking it seriously and how the second shot—the official one —had been much more somber. The one I was looking at now was the first photo, the one that shouldn't exist. I'd thought it had been destroyed.

I carefully tucked the photo into my pocket and turned my back on the shelves, my heart pounding. This made no sense. Emily might have been here as a child, but a photo from *this year*? How? If they got this, what else might they have?

I glanced back toward the office. I had seen the cassette tapes, but no tape player. If they'd got this picture of Emily, was it possible they had recordings too? But if they did, when would she have spoken? And why had she been calling out to me?

The questions swirled, but one thing was clear—I needed to find her now.

I tried to shake off the unsettling feeling creeping over me, forcing myself to focus as I stepped back into the office. The door now looked like a door, not just a seamless part of the wall, and it was messing with my head. If I couldn't find a tape player in here, then maybe I was wrong. Maybe Emily was fine—safe somewhere else, away from this madhouse. I should get out of here before the walls decided to vanish or the furniture started shifting on its own.

I rummaged through the drawers, rifling past loose papers, stray pens, and files for other patients, hoping for some clue that could ground me in reality. Just as I was about to abandon the search and tear apart the office, my eyes landed on the drawer where I'd found Emily's file. Something gnawed at me, a distant itch in the back of my mind.

Then it hit me—this drawer, this room... I *had* been here before. I couldn't have been more than a little boy. I could almost see the dim light slanting through the blinds, casting long shadows across the floor. I remembered a man in a white coat; his back turned as he rifled through the same drawer, muttering something I couldn't understand. I'd watched from the doorway, too scared to move, my small hands gripping the frame. The smell of antiseptic and dust filled the air, and that same unsettling cold crept back into my bones.

The memory faded as quickly as it had come, but its weight lingered. I wasn't imagining things. This wasn't just a coincidence. This office had been part of my life long before today—before Emily.

My hand hovered over the drawer, instinct guiding me more than reason. Slowly, I pulled it open. The drawer creaked, and inside was an old, bulky cassette player. A thick layer of dust covered it, but an unmarked tape sat snugly in the slot, ready to play.

"It's going to be fine," I whispered to myself, though my voice cracked. It wasn't the truth, but I had to convince myself of it. I could still fix this. I could find Emily. We could escape.

With shaking hands, I reeled the tape. Whatever was recorded on it was short, and that should've been reassuring. It wasn't.

I pressed play.

"H-Harold? Harold. Harold, please. Help me. Harold. Ple—"

Emily's voice was abruptly cut off as I slammed my fist into the tape player. I barely felt the sharp edges of the metal cutting into my knuckles. I couldn't move—I just stood there, numb, staring at the cracked player. Her desperate words echoed in my head, each driving deeper into my chest like a knife.

None of this made sense. Why would anyone target Emily? What had they done to make her plead like that? And how had the tape even been placed here? I wasn't an expert on tape players, but there was no way the tape could play from a distance. Which meant someone had physically been here, in this room.

But where had they gone?

The sickening realization crept over me like a shadow. Whoever had played that tape had been here—probably watching me. Maybe they were still nearby, lurking. What kind of person enjoys making someone beg like that? Listening to them plead?

My chest tightened as a cold sweat formed at the back of my neck. I slowly pulled my hand away from the player, staring at the blood-speckled cracks. The damage didn't matter; I didn't need to hear the tape again. Emily's voice was burned into my memory now, and there hadn't been a scream.

That meant she was still here. Somewhere in this twisted place,

Emily was alive. I had let myself get sidetracked by this damn office and the recording.

Without a second thought, I bolted from the office, my heart pounding. But everything had changed. The lights had gone out, plunging the space into near darkness, and the tables had been shoved to the sides, clearing space for a massive symbol drawn across the floor. It was the same one I'd seen before, but now it was larger and more defined.

I took a steadying breath, my mind struggling to make sense of the sudden rush of fragmented memories clawing their way to the surface. This place—it wasn't just unfamiliar. Somewhere deep inside, I knew it. Faint flashes of being here as a child started to resurface—memories I hadn't even realized I'd buried. I couldn't have been over three or four, but the oppressive, suffocating feeling that something was wrong pressed down on me, just as it had back then.

This sanatorium wasn't just some random, abandoned facility—it was part of my past, my childhood. And the more I stood here, the more I realized my connection to this place was far stronger, far darker than I'd ever imagined.

But I couldn't let myself get lost in that now. Emily was still out there. Whatever dark history tied me to this place—tied *us* to this place—could wait. She couldn't. I needed to find her, and I didn't have time to think about anything else.

Turning toward the second door, the one against the far wall, I fought to keep it together. The panic was clawing at me, but I couldn't afford to break down now. Not when I was so close.

Emily was in here somewhere, and we were getting the fuck out of this nightmare.

And after that, I'd make sure this place burned to the ground.

CHAPTER 4

The Locket's Mysteries

I combed through the first floor, desperately searching for any sign of where Emily might be. The rooms fluctuated wildly between pristine order and complete chaos. The nurses' station, next to the head doctor's office, seemed almost normal. Six beds lined the room, each made up with fresh sheets, with a medical cabinet neatly positioned beside them. But stepping into the kitchen was like entering a nightmare; the countertops were littered with rotting meat and scattered bones, as if a feral pack had ransacked the place, devouring anything in sight.

I braced myself as I pushed open the door to the dining room, half-expecting something sinister. The lights blazed overhead, illuminating a long table draped in a pristine white cloth adorned with tiny pots of fake foliage—an unsettling contrast to the horror surrounding it.

The other side of the building offered no reprieve. Shredded papers littered the library floor while red markings marred the shelves, a silent warning of some unseen threat. Yet, the circular storeroom connected to the back of the library remained untouched—board games, books, blankets, and pillows sat there in eerie silence as if waiting for a time that would never come.

The unsettling truth began to dawn on me: There was nowhere for Emily to hide—not from her captor nor from the chilling presence that had pressed play on the tape. As I moved toward the last door in the main room, a sudden crash jolted me from my thoughts. I spun around to see the door to the head doctor's office flung wide open, the desk toppled over, and papers scattered like autumn leaves —a familiar chaos that stirred something deep within me.

I quickly glanced inside, my heart racing, but the office was empty. It was the same office I remembered from my childhood—my original sanctuary and prison—a place that seemed to harbor dark secrets. My gaze darted to the wall where I had discovered the hidden bedroom door. Panic surged through me as I realized it was flat now; there was no indent, no knob, no warm spot, or trace of dust left behind. It was as if the entire room had never existed, leaving me adrift in uncertainty.

"Of course," I muttered, a laugh escaping my lips that held more madness than mirth. "OF FUCKING COURSE!"

Driven by frustration, I whirled around and kicked the desk, splintering wood beneath my foot. "Because why the hell not?"

An unsettling energy surged within me, and I found myself unable to contain the laughter that bubbled up, twisted and wild. "Why should any of this make sense?"

My hands trembled, itching for release, and I fell to my knees, unleashing my fury on everything around me—the desk, the floor, even my legs.

"Disappearing doors!" I shouted, feeling the wood crack under my blows.

"Disappearing people!" I let out a scream as the jagged splinters dug into my skin, worsening the cuts from my earlier encounter with the tape.

"NOTHING MAKES SENSE!" My voice erupted in a raw, primal scream.

When the storm of rage finally subsided, I found myself surrounded by a wreckage of broken wood and splattered blood. My hands bore witness to my chaos, streaked with varying shades of red—a pinkish hue from impending bruises and a deep crimson flowing from the fresh cuts.

I struggled to stand, my legs betraying me, forcing me to lean against the wreckage I'd created as I fought for steady breaths. After my outburst, I knew I should analyze what had set me off. It was something I'd learned in therapy: understanding the root of the impulse was key to overcoming it. But the thought of sitting down for a self-reflective session felt far too overwhelming at this moment.

I reached for the shards of wood, shifting them back and forth in my trembling hands. The splintered edges scraped against my skin, grounding me in the present moment. I focused on the sensations: the sharp pain radiating from my cuts, the dull cramp in my legs from sitting too long, and the coldness of the wood pressing against my palm. Each sensation pulled me back from the brink of panic.

Taking a shaky breath, I turned my attention to my surroundings, forcing myself to identify five things I could see. There was the weathered filing cabinet against the far wall, the stained floor beneath my feet, my legs, the wreckage of the desk, and—wait—a glint of metal among the debris. My heart raced as I recognized the familiar chain of a necklace.

Hadn't I searched the desk earlier? My fingers fumbled as I tried to pull the necklace free, but something large was snagged within the tight space. I traced the crack with my finger, searching for a way to pry it open, but the line was unnaturally straight—too perfect. I realized this line had been there before my violent outburst. Finally, with determination, I found a spot to wedge my fingernail beneath the crack and pulled, revealing a hidden compartment.

Inside lay a bronze oval locket adorned with a tiny knob shaped like wings. The intricate design on one side was too faint to decipher, its lines thin and delicate. As I ran my fingertip over it, some of my blood seeped into the engraving, staining the surface a dark crimson.

Now, the design was more visible. Curly lines framed what seemed to be a flower—a straight line spiraling upward with a second line coiling around it, small circles forming triangles along the path. The top of the first line bore what resembled layers of petals intricately arranged in an egg shape.

The locket warmed in my hand, almost as if it pulsed with life. I pressed the winged knob, hoping it would spring open, but it remained stubbornly shut. Leaning against the wall, I felt an unexpected weight pulling me down. Out of the corner of my eye, I glimpsed the dark wood of a door frame. I chuckled softly; somehow, the hidden bedroom was back.

After a moment's pause, I pushed myself up and headed to the nurses' room. To my relief, it remained untouched. The medical cabinets stood intact. I hurried to the one nearest the door, my heart pounding as I pulled at the handle—locked. The keyhole seemed to taunt me, daring me to open it.

Suddenly, a burning sensation ignited in my palm. I gasped and looked down—the locket glowed a deep red, a faint hissing sound filling the air. With a loud pop, the locket returned to its normal hue, and the cabinet door creaked open slightly.

In disbelief, I hung the chain around my neck, the weight settling comfortably against my skin. I had to focus on tending to my wounds first.

It took a struggle to extract the splinters embedded in my hand, the sting sharp with each tug. I grimaced but pressed on, finally turning my attention to the cream. It had expired by twenty years, but I reasoned it was better than nothing as I rubbed it into my cuts. The stinging made me grit my teeth, but I kept going until my hands were mostly coated. I bandaged my wounds, leaving just a few wraps in the box.

With my injuries taken care of, I turned back to the locket. Logically, it made no sense for it to have caused the cabinet to open, yet I couldn't shake the feeling that it had. Denying the reality of the shifting rooms, the vanishing people, and the walls that concealed doors was becoming increasingly futile.

Lifting the locket to my lips, I whispered, "If you're guiding me, then please lead me to Emily."

For a fleeting moment, the locket pulsed with warmth, and then the left side pressed against my neck as if an unseen force was tugging the chain toward the door.

I drew a shaky breath, compelled to follow its pull. It guided me through the main room, back up the stairs, and down the hall to the door I had first emerged from. As soon as my hand brushed the handle, the chain turned ice cold, the pendant pressing firmly against my chest. The moment I let go, the locket radiated warmth once more.

"Okay, so I can't just waltz in?" I murmured to myself, frustration creeping in. I removed the necklace, scrutinizing it as I tried to decipher its purpose. Earlier, simply thinking about unlocking the cabinet had seemed enough, and asking it to guide me to Emily had led me here. But if I wasn't meant to enter, then what was I supposed to do?

Closing my eyes, I inhaled deeply, grounding myself. I needed to remain calm.

In a moment of instinct, I pressed the locket against the door handle. A wave of warmth flooded my body, settling in my stomach and igniting a spark of hope. Turning the handle, I stepped inside.

Before my eyes even opened, I could sense the room had transformed. A sweet, fruity fragrance replaced the familiar stench of decay. Sunlight streamed in from somewhere, warming my skin.

When I finally dared to look around, I gasped in astonishment. I stood in a vibrant greenhouse. Tables were brimming with lush plants, their greens, reds, oranges, and yellows creating a riot of color. The warm hues of the flowers contrasted sharply with the deep blue blankets spread out on the floor. Across the room, an open door beckoned, leading to the outside, where a table and chair sat invitingly.

"Emily?" I called out, my voice echoing in the stillness. The door slammed shut behind me. "Are you here?"

The only response was the cheerful chirping of birds outside.

Sinking onto the blanket, I stared at the locket, the weight of it pressing heavily into my palm. A part of me screamed to hurl it away, to bury it deep in the earth and forget it ever existed. But instead, I slipped the locket back on and rose to my feet.

Nothing about the sanatorium made sense; I had reached my breaking point once. I couldn't navigate these twisted halls and save Emily on my own. I needed to place my trust in something, and the locket seemed like the only ally I had left. I had asked it to take me to Emily, and it had delivered me here—this had to mean something. I had to trust that, somehow, this place held the key to unraveling the mystery of her disappearance.

CHAPTER 5

Emily's True Agenda

I began my exploration by examining the plants, but there was little to uncover. Orange anemones intertwined with red lilies and yellow roses, creating an odd bouquet of color. It was surreal how each flower could bloom from the same stalk. Tiny water droplets clung to the leaves and petals, yet as I scanned the greenhouse, I found no sign of a watering can.

The blanket in the center of the room offered no secrets, either. Its soft fabric bore a comforting earthy scent, but there was nothing concealed within its folds. Still, as I made my way toward the exit, I succumbed to the urge to wrap it around my shoulders, seeking a semblance of warmth amid the unsettling atmosphere.

Stepping outside, I found the grass dotted with clusters of narcissus flowers. Despite the trees surrounding the sanatorium, none loomed here—only a small, circular table that seemed meant for a child rather than an adult. Two chairs had been shoved aside, their surfaces cluttered with picture books and drawings. I reached for the top sheet, intrigued.

The drawing depicted two figures—one a boy with black hair, the other a blonde girl. They stood hand in hand in a grassy field, surrounded by what seemed to be oversized orange cats, their whimsical presence contrasting sharply with the somber surroundings.

I placed the drawing back on the stack and shifted my gaze to the empty table. Thin lines carved into its surface formed an H shape. Curious, I placed my hands on either side of the middle line and pushed. The panels slid apart easily, revealing a chaotic jumble of papers, notebooks, and tapes.

I reached for the tapes first, their labels identical to those I had discovered in the head doctor's office. Each bore the designation for patient number 0203031945-05271947, recorded between May 27, 1947, and June 10, 1950. At the end of each label was EW01 or EW05.

My finger traced one of the labels, a desperate urge to know more clawing at my insides. But unless I wanted to haul them back to the head doctor's office in hopes the tape player still functioned, I was stuck. Setting the tapes aside, I turned to the loose papers.

They appeared to be letters—short and written in an elegant, looping script. Each bore the same sign-off: "From, Evelyn." Some were crumpled and battered, while others looked freshly penned.

One caught my eye, torn in half but hastily reattached.

Apply again next year. We'll make sure you get accepted.

Do not fail.

From, Evelyn.

Another letter bore a deep crease from countless folds.

You've done well. We'll let you take the lead from here.

Congratulations.

From, Evelyn.

I unfolded yet another letter and felt my breath hitch. The contents were mundane—another note from Evelyn asking if the recipient needed anything else. But a familiar scrawl at the bottom drew my attention: Emily had written yesterday's date along the edge of the page: July 15, 1972.

Desperation surged as I spread out the other letters, scanning for any sign of Emily's name or handwriting, but there was none. That left the notebooks.

I chuckled lightly, opening the first one to a random page. The ink had smudged as if a hand had brushed across it while writing, but there was no mistaking the handwriting. It was Emily's. A glance at the other three notebooks confirmed they all belonged to her. But I had never seen her with any of them.

What had she been doing here? What secrets did these books hold? The weight of uncertainty settled heavily on my shoulders as I pondered my next move.

My fingers brushed against the locket. "Is this what you were hoping I would discover?"

A Narcissus Flower is a symbol of hope and joy

With a heavy heart, I turned my attention to the notebooks, discovering they were diaries. They chronicled Emily's life at Chapel Hill, each entry a fleeting glimpse into her day-to-day—the mundane rhythm of classes, assignments, and what she had eaten. It wasn't until I reached the middle of the first diary, when our paths had crossed, that the entries began to expand. A warmth spread through me as I read about the start of our relationship—how she had bravely approached me for a group project, those long nights spent poring over books, and the time I had gotten too nervous to ask her out and accidentally overindulged in wine.

My cheeks flushed as I lingered on the last entry.

He kissed me tonight. I wasn't expecting it. But he did. We're dating now.

I set the diary aside, my heart racing, and moved on to the next one.

This diary had entries dated from the present year. Instead of chronicling her experiences, they detailed my struggle to find a job and the toll it had taken on me. At first, I found it endearing—Emily had noticed my hidden anguish amid a wave of rejections. Yet, as I read further, an unsettling shift occurred. Each entry became more terse, more urgent, reflecting her mounting frustration as I secured more interviews and prospects.

A stark transformation hit after the entry, marking the day I landed my job two months ago. Instead of the usual recounting of daily life, her notes turned into a jarring account of her experiences at the sanatorium. At first, I assumed they were just notes for her dissertation, but the content was far from academic. She meticulously described the physical structure of the building, detailing rooms and peculiar observations, including the letters I had found etched into the walls and even the plants thriving in the greenhouse behind me.

The final page revealed a chilling list of personal items: her old sweater, the earrings she never took off, a recently purchased hat, and her green notebook. The last item was circled, accompanied by a small note that read:

Place in car?

In the corner, another note was underlined three times:

Have them call in the morning. Play tape.

I set the diary down, my pulse racing. The only tape containing Emily's voice that I could recall was in the recorder, its case cracked and forgotten. But why would she record it? What purpose could it serve?

Her notebook was in the car parked outside. If she had indeed done that, then wouldn't it make sense she would have arranged for the call to be made as well? There could be another tape—something that didn't involve her pleading for help.

I pressed the diary tightly against my chest, the locket's chill seeping into my sternum. My eyes returned to the children's drawings scattered among the picture books, a knot forming in my stomach as I recognized them—they could easily be depictions of Emily and me. A surge of anger coursed through me; I wanted to rip them apart, to see the fragments dance in the air and be swallowed by the Earth, forgotten forever.

I yearned to scream, to cry, to erase the heavy burden of all I had uncovered.

Instead, I took a steady breath and rose to my feet. The blanket slipped off my shoulders, and I quickly spread it out on the ground beside me. After a moment of fumbling, I folded it into the triangle shape I needed to use as a makeshift backpack. With the first diary —the one chronicling the beginning of our relationship—secured inside, I slung the bag over my shoulder and headed back toward the greenhouse.

A laugh escaped me as I stared at the doorless back wall. Bringing the locket to my lips, I whispered my command, "Reveal the door."

For a heartbeat, nothing happened. I tried again. "Lead me out of here... Take me back... Exit?"

The locket bounced lightly against my chest as I let it drop. No matter what I said, there was no shift in the surroundings or in the locket's response. I was clearly overlooking something.

I laid the blanket back in the center of the room and glanced around, but there was still nothing to see. Returning the diary to the table didn't yield any results either. Not that the locket didn't want me to take anything from the room; it felt like there was a deeper layer to this. I approached the wall, feeling along the surface in search of any sign that a hidden door had simply gone invisible like the one in the bedroom. But there was nothing.

Pulling the necklace off, I lifted it to eye level. "What am I missing? What do you need from me?"

"It's not about what it needs. It's about what you desire."

I spun around to find a small child—no older than four—watching me from the greenhouse door. A single glance at him revealed something was off. He was alarmingly thin, his skin pale with dark shadows beneath his eyes. His black hair hung in greasy strands, and his hospital-like garb was smeared with green and brown stains. My heart sank as I noticed he wasn't wearing any shoes, like the child I'd seen crawling through the window.

As I stepped closer, the boy's eyes widened, and he retreated slightly. I crouched down, lifting my hands to show I meant no harm. His gaze fell on my bandaged hands, but he seemed undeterred. His shoulders relaxed a fraction, and he approached me cautiously.

Once he settled in front of me, I lowered my hands. "What's your name?"

The boy pointed to the locket. "It does what you want."

"Excuse me?"

"It listens. You just need to ask it the right way."

I frowned. "Do you know much about the locket?"

"Not really. Just as much as you do." His eyes locked onto mine with an intensity that sent a chill down my spine. "It wants what you want. What you truly desire."

"And... what is that?"

"To stay, Harold." A wide grin stretched across his face, unnatural yet strangely innocent. Instead of revealing any discomfort, he erupted into laughter.

My heart raced. I felt an urge to laugh along with him, but I fought it down, pressing my fist against my lips to stifle the impulse.

The boy slumped forward, and a mix of tears and snot began to stream down his face.

I bit my hand, focusing on the pain. It was grounding—forcing me to remain present instead of succumbing to the chaotic emotions threatening to spill over. From his position on the floor, the boy looked up at me. Despite his laughter, his lips curled into a frown, and his brows knitted together in distress.

After a brief pause, he rested his head on the floor, his laughter intertwining with soft cries for help. "Please. Help me. Please."

"It's okay," I said once I found my composure. "I'll figure this out. I promise."

CHAPTER 6

Shadows of the Mind

The first thing I needed to do was ground the kid. His hysterical laughter echoed through the empty space, far too loud and too unnatural for comfort. I didn't know what had triggered it, but if focusing on the present had saved me from losing it, I hoped it could save him, too. The only problem was that I had no idea how to pull him out of whatever had its grip on him.

His head was down, his face hidden, and I couldn't get him to look at me or respond to anything I said. Touch was an option, but I had no clue how he'd react if a stranger like me laid hands on him. He could panic, maybe lash out, or worse, spiral even further.

There was no food around, nothing I could use to ground him with taste, but then my eyes landed on the old blanket I had thrown on the floor. Without overthinking it, I grabbed it and wrapped it around his shoulders.

"Hey, kid. Deep breaths. Come on." My voice wavered, but I kept talking. "Focus on now. Focus on what's real. Deep breaths. You're okay."

The laughter didn't stop right away, but it started to soften, fading little by little. I stayed there, speaking softly, until the only sound left was the boy's shaky breaths. My throat felt raw, but I was relieved to see him finally calm. He was trembling, the fit having drained him.

I scanned the room for something—anything—that could help. There. A cup sat on a table I knew I hadn't seen before.

I didn't question it. "Here," I said, bringing it over. "Drink this. It'll help."

His hands were unsteady as he took the cup and sipped. When he handed it back, I noticed the water level hadn't changed.

"Thank you," he whispered, his voice hoarse.

I nodded, unsure how to respond. After a moment, I set the cup on the floor beside us. "What's your name?" I said, trying to break the silence.

He blinked, looking dazed, before answering. "You can just call me Abi, I suppose."

"Okay, Abi. Are you feeling better?"

"A little." He didn't meet my gaze.

"Think you can stand?" I asked gently. "We need to get moving."

"Why?" His voice quivered, and when our eyes met, I could see the fear buried deep inside them.

"We can't stay here," I said, glancing at the spot where the door used to be. "We have to figure out how to get out of here."

But his grip tightened on my arm, and his face went pale. "Why would we leave? It's safe here."

"Abi—" I paused, unsure how to explain the situation.

"See?" His voice grew frantic. "We should stay. Forever." He scrambled away, grabbing a plate of cookies from nowhere, hands shaking. "We have everything we need here. Just... Please promise we won't leave, Harold."

My blood ran cold. "What did you call me?"

"Harold?" Abi's voice was small, hesitant. But all I could focus on was that word. My name.

"How do you know my name?" I demanded, my heart racing.

"Everyone here knows your name," he mumbled.

My grip tightened on his shoulders. "What do you mean, everyone? Who are they? How do they know me?"

His eyes filled with tears. "Harold, you're hurting me."

"Tell me, Abi!" My voice rose, desperate.

"Stop!"

I looked up, and there, in the doorway of the greenhouse, stood a man. His lanky frame made his arms and legs seem almost too long for the blue knit sweater and jeans he wore. He held himself perfectly straight, and under normal circumstances, it would've made him seem confident—if it weren't for the tears welling in his eyes. His black hair had been shaved to a stubble, but despite that, the resemblance between him and Abi was unmistakable.

"Let him go," the man said quietly, though his words carried an undeniable weight.

As soon as I released his shoulders, Abi darted behind the other man's legs, seeking shelter.

I cleared my throat, turning my gaze away. "I didn't mean to scare you, Abi. I'm sorry."

"It's oka—"

"No, it's not okay!" The man's voice was cutting as he ran a hand over the rough stubble on his chin. "What does 'sorry' fix? You still hurt him! Words, don't undo that!"

"I know, but—"

"But nothing!" He crossed his arms tightly over his chest, his whole body shaking. "You can't undo it. The damage is already done, and now we—"

Abi stepped out from behind the man, standing on his tiptoes to reach his elbow. "It's okay, Ten. I forgive him."

"O-oh." The man—Ten—blinked, momentarily thrown. "I... okay. Sorry, Harold."

"It's fine." I rubbed the back of my neck, tension lingering. "You know who I am too?"

He nodded. "Everyone in Lyaeus knows about Emily and Harold. There's no one who doesn't."

A chill shot through me, but I forced myself to stay calm. I didn't want to scare Abi again. "You know Emily?"

"Absolutely," Abi chimed in, his voice soft yet enthusiastic. "She's the one who helped set up this place for us."

"Do you know where she is now?"

They shared a quick look before Ten replied with a shake of his head. "I'm sorry, but no."

"No, that's... it's not on you," I replied.

I grabbed the cup again, swirling the water idly, trying to calm the storm raging inside me. I stared at the vortex spinning in the cup before downing half the water in one gulp. The absurdity of it hit me, and I let out a small laugh as I set the cup down.

Slamming my hand against the ground, I shot up, grabbing the locket to check its temperature before glaring at the two. "How do I get out of here?"

"No!" Abi's voice trembled, his head shaking violently. "I told you, it's not safe out there!"

"You don't have to come with me. But I need to find Emily."

Ten let out a short, bitter laugh. "So you're just going to leave us behind?"

"I'm not abandoning anyone. I'm doing what I have to do. The choice to stay or leave is yours."

A sharp whistle from behind made me turn. Another figure had appeared, leaning casually against the wall. His face was hidden beneath the hood of a red sweater, but the black hair peeking out suggested he was like the others.

He examined his hand with unnatural stiffness, his voice dripping with sarcasm. "Does it take just one glass of water to make you act like an asshole? I can't say I'm shocked. Nice guy routine doesn't last long, huh?"

Anger tightened in my chest, but I held my ground. "I'm just trying to find Emily."

"Oh, I see. Trying to avoid all the freaky shit going on here, right?" The hooded man pushed off the wall, stalking around me with predatory ease. "That's the reason you're so quick to abandon the kid. You think because he didn't drink the water, he's not real. Just another twisted creation of this place."

Heat rose to my face. "Shut up."

"And if Abi's not real, then neither is Ten, right? You got fooled by this place again, or maybe you're just losing it. You've already thrown logic out the window. Why not—"

I let go of the locket, grabbed the guy's hoodie, and pulled him close, his smug grin confirming my suspicions—he looked just like the others. The only difference was the infuriating smirk.

"I said, shut up."

His grin widened. "Make me."

My free hand tightened into a fist, but the sound of muffled sobs made me hesitate. I glanced toward the door and saw Ten crouched in front of Abi, both of them shaking as they clung to each other.

I pushed the hooded man away, frustration bubbling up inside me. "Then explain this 'logic' to me. When I drank the water, the cup emptied, but when Abi did, it stayed full. Why?"

He shrugged, a mocking grin on his face. "Maybe it's because the two people who actually wanted the water used it? Or perhaps Abi's been here longer and knows the ins and outs of this twisted place, while you, on the other hand, just fumbled around like an idiot? Maybe you just need to get lost!"

I bit my lip, struggling to keep my anger in check. "And how did you all just appear out of thin air?"

"Right, says the guy who just popped up in the greenhouse like he owned the place. Unless..." His smirk widened. "Looks like you're caught up in this twisted game as well, huh? Bet you are!"

"I get it." I buried my head in my hands and let out a shaky breath. "How... how did you know what I was thinking?"

"Because I'm in your head. Or maybe you're just that easy to read?"

Ten groaned softly. "Alright, we get it. Can you just... stop now, Manny?"

The hooded man let out a sharp whistle before retreating to his corner.

"I... I'm sorry," I managed, clearing my throat. "I shouldn't have jumped to conclusions."

Abi wiped his tears, giving me a shaky smile. "It's okay."

"Yeah, I mean," Manny began, fiddling with the hem of his hoodie, "we could still be part of Lyaeus' twisted mess. Yours, or Emily's. Or maybe we're just some random pawns in this game of chess."

I turned back to Ten and Abi. "I mean it, though. I need to leave."

"But," Abi protested, "I keep telling you not to!"

I shook my head, my resolve hardening. "I know. I appreciate your concern. But if Emily's out there, trapped in this chaos, I have to help her."

Manny placed his hand on my shoulder, causing me to flinch. With a casual ease, he flipped through one of the diaries as if the pages were turning themselves. Suddenly, he slammed the book shut, a sharp sound cutting through the tension. "Are you seriously planning to prioritize finding her? You two were close, but doesn't this just make you want to scream?"

I snatched the book from his hands, slamming it down on a nearby table. "There must be a purpose behind all of this."

"Oh? And you're just going to crawl back to her, taking whatever crap she throws at you?" Manny chuckled before suddenly covering his mouth with his fist, his eyes wide with surprise. He took several breaths, and when he finally moved his hand, he looked as calm as before the outburst. "Do what you want, I guess."

"It's not what you want, though!" Abi shouted. "If it were, the door wouldn't be gone. Stay here, Harold! Please!"

I glanced down at the locket, remembering Manny's earlier words. "You brought that up earlier... so the locket believes I'd prefer to remain here?"

"Where it's safe. Where you don't have to deal with all this weird stuff anymore."

I kneeled to Abi's level. "I think I understand. The locket believes I'm scared."

I pulled the locket off and held it up, its bronze surface catching the sunlight and gleaming with a warm glow. As I held it, the metal began to warm against my palm.

"But here's the thing. Even if I'm scared, what I really want is to find Emily. I need to understand what she's been up to, figure out the connection with the diaries and the tapes, and uncover the truth about this place. I can't do that if I remain here. So, I'm leaving."

A strange sensation settled in my stomach as a faint clicking sound echoed in the air. Turning around, I was startled to see the door I'd entered swing open, revealing the dim office of the sanatorium. I stood up, determination surging through me, and stepped into the corridors of Lyaeus, leaving everything behind.

CHAPTER 7

Forgotten Memories

I had barely stepped into the hallway when I halted. My gaze flicked around, but everything remained unchanged since my last visit.

"So, what's the plan? Just wandering aimlessly?" I spun around at the voice, startled to find Manny a few steps behind me. He grinned, folding his arms across his chest. "That little pep talk was charming, but you can't shake us off that easily."

My eyes flicked past him to where Ten cradled Abi, the boy's face buried against his shoulder. I tried to catch Ten's gaze, but his eyes were busy scanning the chaos surrounding us.

Manny snapped his fingers in front of me, bringing my focus back. "So, got any bright ideas?"

"The... the locket—"

"Right, the locket. It's going to lead you to a magical garden when you ask it about Emily again. Do you honestly believe that's the right approach?"

I inhaled deeply. "Do you have a better suggestion?"

"Do I look like someone who brainstorms ideas?" Manny shrugged dismissively.

Before I could retort, Ten cleared his throat. "There are plenty of places to explore. We just need to look. Where haven't you gone yet?"

A queasy feeling settled in my stomach as I thought of the shadowy figure ascending the tower. "Most of the second floor and the towers."

"Just that?"

"It's a good place to start."

Ten raised an eyebrow but remained silent. He simply nodded and moved past me.

With no other options, I followed Ten as he led the way down the corridor, past the stairs, and toward the back tower.

Some depicted those enormous cats, while others illustrated people caught in motion. Painted in the same unsettling red, the lines were chaotic—some shaky, others extending unnecessarily long.

I was so engrossed in a drawing of two intertwined figures I almost missed Ten stopping at one of the doors. I would have walked right by if not for his knocking.

Instead of opening it, Ten adjusted Abi in his arms and waited.

"I don't think—" I started, but before I could finish, the door swung open, spilling warm light into the hallway.

A woman stood there, seeming around my age. Fine lines had etched themselves at the corners of her eyes and across her forehead. Her long hair hung in disarray, and her dress looked equally neglected. I tried to discern more details, but she seemed to fade in and out of focus. She wasn't transparent, but the more I tried to fixate on her, the less certain I became of her presence.

"Ah, children." Her voice drifted toward me, distant as if she were speaking from the far end of a cavern, but I could still detect its rough texture. "What can I—"

Harsh coughs interrupted her, making me wince. Without thinking, I stepped forward and gently placed my hand on her shoulder, guiding her inside. "Sorry to intrude, Ms. Pachi."

"Not at all. I'm always pleased to have—" Another fit of coughs shook her, causing her frame to tremble. Once it subsided, she continued, "It's nice to have company."

I helped her to the bed, urging her to sit. "You need to rest."

"I'm not that bad yet."

"Still—" I applied gentle pressure to her shoulders, coaxing her to lie back. She felt neither warm nor cold, as if I were touching a lifeless doll instead of a person. "The doctors said overexerting yourself will only worsen your condition."

Ms. Pachi smiled, and for a fleeting moment, I felt like I could gaze at her without fear of her vanishing. "It's wonderful to see you again, Harold, dear."

"You too." I took the edge of the blanket and draped it over her. "Now, sleep."

I blinked, and in an instant, she had vanished. The bed and blanket were replaced by a rusted frame, and the soft light that had greeted me was gone. A sense of discomfort twisted in my stomach.

I spun around and shot an icy glare at the three figures hovering in the doorway. "What the hell was that?"

Manny let out a low whistle. "Looks like someone's—"

"Shut it... Ten?"

Ten handed Abi to Manny before stepping into the room. "You knew her."

"I've never met her."

"But you knew her name. You knew what the doctors said."

I tightened my fist, anger boiling beneath the surface, but Manny interrupted with a teasing laugh. "I can see it in his eyes—he's really itching to land a punch, Ten!"

"Enough!" I snapped.

"I'd say 'make me,' but I'm holding the kid, so..."

My gaze landed on Abi, who was trembling, clutching Manny's hoodie so tightly that his knuckles were white. I bit my lip and sighed.

"Sorry," Ten whispered. "I just... needed you to see that."

"Why?"

"To make things easier." He rubbed a hand over his stubbled chin. "You keep dodging it, Harold. I understand, but you need to face it. You've been here before."

"No. I haven't."

Ten studied me for a moment, then shook his head and turned toward the hallway. Part of me wanted to stay and argue, but I followed him, with Manny and Abi close behind.

When Ten reached the staircase—the one where I had seen the shadowy figure earlier—he shot me a crooked smile. "Last chance."

For the first time since we left the room, Abi looked up, pleading. "Ten, please…"

Ignoring him, Ten ascended the stairs. I instinctively tried to step back to escape this impending doom, but a hand landed on my back. Manny leaned over my shoulder, his voice low. "If you've really never been here before, then what's the big deal? Nothing will happen if you just go up those stairs."

I bit my lip. He had a point; if the shadowy figure I had glimpsed was a figment of my imagination or harmless like Ms. Pachi, then avoiding the treatment room was irrational.

With every step upward, my terror intensified. Each footfall shrank me down, like a child approaching their teacher for a reprimand. I tried to slow my pace, hoping to delay the inevitable, but my legs betrayed me, propelling me forward.

At some point, I heard Abi cry.

When I reached the top of the tower, Ten had vanished. All that stood before me was the imposing metal door towering over me. I had to stand on my tiptoes to grasp the handle and stumbled slightly as I pushed the door open.

As the door creaked open, the sterile scent of antiseptic flooded my senses, transporting me back to a dark corner of my past. The circular chamber that lay beyond resembled a sinister laboratory, conjuring memories I had buried deep within. Strange, unfamiliar medical instruments surrounded an operating table, their gleaming surfaces mocking the grim scene that unfolded before me in my mind.

A white sheet draped over a woman revealed a disturbing crimson stain at its center, a harrowing sign of her condition. My heart raced as a choked cry escaped my lips, and I dashed toward the table, my legs feeling smaller and weaker, just as they had when I was a child. A nearby cart cluttered with bloodied scalpels and pliers wobbled precariously, and I instinctively scrambled up, using the cart as leverage to hoist myself onto the table.

Her long, chestnut hair spilled behind her like a dark waterfall. Her face wore a peaceful expression as if she were merely asleep. I placed my hands on her bare shoulders and gasped at the icy chill that coursed through me. "Wake up, Mommy. Please." Tears streamed down my cheeks, splattering onto her face, yet she remained unresponsive. She always came when I cried—scooping me into her warm embrace, letting me bury my face in her comforting shoulders.

Suddenly, arms encircled me, pulling me away. I struggled, twisting and kicking, even biting and screaming, but the nurse was too strong. She dragged me toward the door, my small hands reaching out in vain, desperate to grasp my mother and rouse her from this nightmare.

But the door slammed shut behind us, sealing off any hope, leaving only the echoes of a childhood trauma I had tried so hard to forget.

I drew a shaky breath, my body quivering as nausea threatened to overwhelm me. I pressed my back against the cold wall; the weight of the moment was almost too much to bear. Surrounding me were the three boys: Abi clinging to my legs, while Manny and Ten flanked me, their presence oddly comforting yet not enough to chase away the chill that enveloped us.

I wiped my face, trying to erase the evidence of tears and snot, before finally lifting my gaze. Even in my crouched position, the metal door was smaller than I remembered.

The locket against my chest radiated warmth, a strange contrast to the icy fear creeping through me.

"What just happened?" I whispered, my voice trembling.

"It was a memory," Ten replied softly, leaning into me for support.

"But I..." My mind drifted back to the memories of my tiny hands and legs. "I don't remember my mother."

"Technically, you still don't," Manny interjected, only to receive a gentle shove from Ten. "I'm just saying..."

"She was kind," Abi said, his voice barely above a whisper.

I placed a hand on Abi's head, smoothing down his hair. "You knew her?"

Abi hummed affirmatively. A surge of questions flooded my mind, but when I glanced at Manny and Ten, they simply shook their heads, their exhaustion mirroring my own.

Leaning my head against the wall, I shut my eyes, trying to sift through the chaotic memories. But all I could conjure was her face —eyes closed, yet I could almost envision them: warm brown orbs that sparkled with laughter. The thought tightened my chest, compelling me to clutch the locket tighter.

"I think I need a moment."

Ten nodded. "Take your time."

As if choreographed, they shifted away, creating a space for me to escape down the stairs to the second floor. I descended, my feet moving on autopilot. It wasn't until the sunlight warmed my face that I finally regained a semblance of control and took in my surroundings.

Cushioned benches were arranged in neat rows at the center of the room, and the walls were glass, granting a stunning view of the seemingly endless maze of trees outside. Dark green pines jutted against the bright blue sky. Approaching the windows, I spotted my car outside, parked awkwardly against the remnants of the surrounding fence. The sight of the other car still there reassured me—Emily had to be nearby.

As I turned, I noticed a glass door amid the windows leading to a small garden. Unlike the wild chaos below, this one was meticulously tended, brimming with fruits and vegetables, each plant standing in its gravel plot, perfectly aligned.

I stepped forward, ready to explore the garden, when a movement caught my eye. A flash of blonde hair darted down the stairs at the other end of the hallway.

In an instant, I was running, propelled by a desperate need to reach her before she vanished again. Her name escaped my lips, urgency driving me forward. "Emily!"

CHAPTER 8

The Illusion of Emily

The sharp sound of a door slamming echoed just before I reached the bottom of the stairs. My gaze swept the main room, where every door stood wide open except for the one leading to the head doctor's office. I fixated on the wooden barrier; its silence was heavy with unspoken dread. The thought of opening it only to find the room as empty as before pulled me down like a leaden weight.

I reached for the handle, but a wave of nausea twisted in my stomach. I pressed a hand against my abdomen, inhaling deeply to push through the discomfort. Then I caught her voice echoing from the library. "Harold?"

Looking up, I half-expected the hallway to be empty, but there she was, framed in the doorway of the library, a soft glow from behind casting her in light. A gentle smile graced her lips, and she looked just as she had all those years ago. I wanted to dash toward her, to bridge the gap between us, but all I could do was stand frozen in place, captivated by the sight of her.

Suddenly, I was back in that moment—the memory vivid and alive. My heart raced as I gazed up at the restaurant sign—Taverna. Emily had picked this spot, and despite the pinch it put on my wallet, I was more than willing to treat her. I wanted our first date to be perfect, especially after the awkward moment when I'd impulsively kissed her, and she revealed she hadn't realized it was supposed to be a date. Mortified, I couldn't stop apologizing until she took my hand and asked me to be her boyfriend., and she revealed she hadn't realized it was supposed to be a date. Mortified, I couldn't stop apologizing until she took my hand and asked me to be her boyfriend.

Taking a deep breath, I pushed open the door and scanned the room. It didn't take long to spot her at a table in the back. Her hair was elegantly styled in a braided bun, and her makeup was flawlessly done. While other women donned vibrant dresses with daring necklines, Emily looked like she had stepped out of a library. Her white, plaited dress paired with a green floral blouse fell to her knees, and her long pine-colored socks added a unique touch.

I adjusted the collar of my rented suit jacket, suddenly questioning my attire, when Emily caught sight of me. Her smile lit up the room. She leaped from her seat, rushing over to snatch the flowers from my hand.

"You came!" she exclaimed.

"Of course I did," I stammered.

She laughed softly, a sound that sent warmth through me. Without breaking eye contact, she took my hand and led me back to our table. "I hope you don't mind, but I ordered for us."

I fought the urge to wince. My plan had been to choose the least expensive dish on the menu. "That's fine."

"By the way, I came up with an idea," she mentioned as we got comfortable. I leaned forward, captivated by her presence, as she continued, "After dinner, why don't we grab a bottle of wine and head back to your place?", as she continued, "After dinner, why don't we grab a bottle of wine and head back to your place?"

My cheeks burned at the suggestion. The thought both thrilled and terrified me. "Sounds good," I replied, hoping I didn't sound as nervous as I felt.

But just as I lost myself in the memory of Emily's laughter and the warmth of her presence, her voice rang out, pulling me back to the here and now. "Harold!" Emily's voice rang out, pulling me from my thoughts as she dashed toward me, her plaited white dress billowing like a soft cloud behind her. I instinctively reached for her, but she halted just out of my grasp, a mix of joy and urgency in her eyes. "You came... Of course, you did.", you did."

A thousand questions swirled in my mind, but I knew there was one I had to ask first. "Are you okay?"

"I... will be." Her words trembled, and as I stepped closer, she instinctively stepped back.

"Emily?"

"Harold, there's something important you need to know."

Before I could process her words, she turned and sprinted back into the library. I followed with confusion clouding my thoughts. The room was transformed; the chaos was gone. The scattered papers had been cleared away, and the shelves were lined with books instead of strange symbols. At the back, near the door to the storage room, stood Emily, waiting for me. confusion clouding my thoughts. The room was transformed; the chaos was gone. The scattered papers had been cleared away, and the shelves were lined with books instead of strange symbols. At the back, near the door to the storage room, stood Emily, waiting for me.

"You need to know. But..." She hesitated, her gaze scanning me from head to toe. "I don't think... you can handle... the truth yet."

"The truth—? I—?" I shook my head, frustration rising. "Forget that for a second. Are you sure you're alright? You sound winded."

"It's easier... as a child. But you... you want to see this."

With that, Emily turned and, placing one hand at the center of the door and the other on the handle, opened it. What I expected to be a circular storage room instead revealed a narrow, rectangular space crammed with floor-to-ceiling cabinets. They stood tightly packed, creating a maze of wood. Each drawer was labeled, but the organization eluded me. The deeper I followed Emily into the labyrinth, the more I felt I might get lost in the chaos without her guidance.

When we finally paused, she opened a drawer marked "A.M." and pulled out two files: one for Adam Morgan and the other for Adelaide Morgan. My heart sank. I recognized those names; the director of the orphanage had mentioned them when I was ten, but I'd brushed it off—they had been dead long.

The man's face in the file was foreign to me; gray hair and a long beard made him unrecognizable. But I had just seen Adelaide, lifeless, on that operating table. My gaze lingered on her picture.

"What are these?" I asked, my voice trembling.

Emily pointed to the string of numbers next to their names. "Patient files."

For reasons I couldn't explain, I began repeating the numbers in my head, trying to memorize them as if they held the key to something I desperately needed to understand.

Adam Morgan, patient number 2807131917-05271947.

Adelaide Morgan, patient number 2510081920-05271947.

Adam Morgan, patient number 2807131917-05271947.

Adelaide Morgan, patient number 2510081920-05271947.

I opened the files, expecting a single page like Emily's, but was met with a flood of information—pages detailing their struggles, treatments, and declines. Both had battled tuberculosis; my father had suffered the typical symptoms, but my mother had endured violent vomiting. And across the top of each page, bold letters screamed, "Keep Away From Harold."

The final page of each file contained their death certificates. The back was marked with various organs, some with checks, others with X's.

I bit my lip until I tasted blood. "I don't understand."

Emily flipped through the pages until she reached their initial assessment. She pointed to the blood types. "They're both… O positive. You're A positive."

My stomach churned, laughter bubbling up unbidden. "So what? I was orphaned twice? What does that even matter? What does any of this even mean?!"

Despite my outburst, a smile tugged at Emily's lips. "No. Your father had a lover. Your real mother. My stepmother… she isn't kind, and she hates him for it… not that she's wrong to."

"I thought you didn't know your parents."

Emily took the files from my trembling hands and returned them to the drawer. When she turned back, her expression had shifted, deepening with intensity. Before I could react, she pressed me against the filing cabinet, leaning in close.

My face flushed. "E-Emily?"

"That's why… You're perfect, Harold. It's why they… chose you." A grin spread across her face, and in an instant, her lips were on mine.

The kiss felt achingly familiar, the taste of wine lingering like a memory of our first date. But when I put my hands on her hips and gently pushed her back, it wasn't the same reason I had that night.

Emily frowned, echoing words from our past. "Was it not to your liking?"

I didn't tell her I wasn't ready like I had before. Instead, my gaze dropped to where my hands rested on her waist, and a pang of recognition shot through me—it felt like when I'd guided Ms. Pachi back to her bed, just a little less hollow, like I had before. Instead, my gaze dropped to where my hands rested on her waist, and a pang of recognition shot through me—it felt like when I'd guided Ms. Pachi back to her bed, just a little less hollow.

"Don't you want this?" she asked, her voice softening.

"That's not…" I slipped past her, running a hand over my neck, searching for calm amid the storm of revelations. Something important felt missing, the air thick with unspoken truths.

I patted down my chest, panic rising when I felt nothing. "Where's the locket?"

Before I could process my anxiety, Emily's arms wrapped around me from behind. "Harold, please, choose me. Choose my madness, not hers."

I spun around, ready to demand an explanation for the chaos swirling around us, but she had vanished. At my feet lay the locket, a faint glow radiating from the metal. As my hand hovered above it, waves of heat pulsed through the air.

Suddenly, the room flickered, the filing cabinets morphing into the circular storage room I had found before. The moment I grasped the necklace, the filing cabinets solidified, trapping me in the maze.

Instead of moving, I traced the intricate design on the locket, fury bubbling beneath the surface. I wanted to hurl it against the wall, to scream until my throat was raw, to rip open every drawer and destroy every document within.

My grip tightened around the locket, the cuts in my palms stretching painfully, the bandages soaking with blood, but I didn't care. I couldn't care. All I could do was laugh, a manic sound that echoed off the walls.

I raised the locket to my eye level, fury boiling over. "WHERE THE FUCK IS SHE?"

Silence swallowed my words. No sign of Emily, real or imagined, appeared around the corner; an oppressive stillness settled in the room as if the world had frozen, determined to withhold any answers.

And then I broke. The locket flew from my hand, crashing against the wall. Pain shot through me as I watched it hit the wall. The storage room reemerged, the locket tumbling to the floor, landing atop a blanket, and kicking up a cloud of dust. I let out a shaky breath and stormed over to a nearby table stacked with games. With a swift motion, I knocked it over, watching as pieces erupt from their boxes, scattering across the floor like a chaotic puzzle.

I kicked the bottom of the table, a scream escaping my lips as pain radiated through my leg—the same foot I'd used to kick down the door. But the pain only fueled my rage. I moved to a shelf, ripping books, papers, and stray pencils from their places, watching them crash to the ground.

As my hands gripped the edge of the empty shelf, I was seconds away from toppling it over when I hesitated. My heart thundered in my chest, my body trembling with adrenaline. Part of me screamed to continue—to shred every inch of the room—but somehow, I pushed that urge down.

Releasing the shelf, I stepped back, forcing myself to breathe. No matter how many calming techniques I tried, the familiar heat coursed through my veins, a wildfire of rage.

Then, a slow clapping echoed through the chaos, making me whirl around, a snarl twisting my lips. Manny emerged, strolling over to the blanket where the locket lay. He picked it up, laughter spilling from his lips like poison.

He turned to face me, a manic grin spreading across his face. My heart stopped as I took in the sight of him—wide eyes gleaming with madness, pointed teeth bared in a predatory smile, and his spine twisted unnaturally, a grotesque caricature of a human.

"Hey, Harold, once you're done with your little outburst, can it be my turn?"

CHAPTER 9

The Hostages Within

Manny began to stalk toward me, his movements stiff and disjointed, like a marionette pulled by invisible strings. My eyes darted around the room, searching for any sign of the others, but it was just the two of us. A tremor coursed through me, though it wasn't fear gripping me. Instead, a strange heat simmered beneath my skin, and the air felt charged with anticipation, like everything was teetering on the edge.

As Manny's fist swung toward me, I willed my body to move, to dodge, but I couldn't. My limbs stayed frozen, leaving me powerless to do anything but watch in eerie detachment as the blow came closer.

Then, suddenly, a different image flashed before my eyes—my hands. Small, trembling. The room around me seemed to blur as something long-buried clawed its way to the surface.

I stared at my hands—they seemed so small for a nine-year-old. Too small to have done the kind of damage I had to Jack's face. The memory of his blood, bright and streaming from his nose, made my stomach twist. I'd been dragged away, still laughing, as his eyes began to swell, the bruises already forming. In that moment, I hadn't wanted to stop. Now, though, I just felt hollow.

The door to the director's office creaked open. I watched as he circled the chair I'd been told to wait in, his tired face somehow even more worn than usual. The lines around his eyes were deeper, and his carefully combed brown hair was disheveled, revealing strands of gray he normally kept hidden.

He leaned against the edge of his desk, folding his arms. "What was it this time, Harold?"

I sniffed. "He wouldn't give me my book back."

"You know what I'm going to ask next."

I lowered my head, the weight of his gaze too much to bear. "No, my reaction wasn't equal to his action. I tried to stop; I really did, but... I just..."

The director sighed softly and placed a hand on my head, ruffling my hair. "You couldn't control it, huh?"

I nodded, ashamed.

"There are only so many chances I can give you, Harold." I winced at his words, bracing for more, but he continued. "So, here's what we'll do. You'll start coming to me for private lessons, and we'll figure this out."

I looked up, my heart racing, but for the first time, it didn't feel like it was about to explode. "Really? Do you think it'll help?"

He gave me a tight, weary smile. "You're not the first person to struggle with this, and you won't be the last. We just need to help you learn how to manage it."

For the first time in a long while, the burning in my veins didn't seem so overwhelming.

I blinked and suddenly realized I was on top of Manny, my knuckles sore and raw. I could have sworn I'd been hitting him for a while, yet his face showed no sign of injury. The air buzzed with the sound of laughter, though I couldn't tell if it was his... or mine.

Biting down hard on my lip, I rolled off him, landing on all fours, staring at the floor. My breath came in ragged bursts, but no matter how hard I tried to steady it, the tension in my chest wouldn't ease.

"What's wrong?" Manny's voice cut through the fog. "Didn't you like what the locket showed you?"

I tried to speak, but my voice was rough, barely forming the words. "Get out of here."

"Not happening." I heard Manny moving behind me, but I didn't have the courage to turn around. A mistake. A heavy hand gripped the back of my head, shoving my face toward the ground.

"Not when I'm finally having some real fun."

"The fuck—" I started, but Manny snarled, cutting me off.

"Shut up!" His hand pressed harder, driving my face further into the cold floor. "You think you can just pummel someone and then start giving orders?"

"I'm sorry," I muttered, half choking on the words.

"Spare me the bullshit." His voice was laced with venom. "No one's here to save you, Harold. Just us... and this." Something dropped into my vision, barely visible, with my cheek mashed against the ground. The pendant—the damned locket. "Think I can make it work without you?"

A wave of nausea slammed into me, and I swallowed hard, fighting back bile as the room spun. I blinked rapidly, but each time, the surroundings shifted—one moment, we were in the storage room; the next, the doctor's office; then the library, and then the hidden greenhouse where I'd first met them. Finally, we landed in the operating room.

But it wasn't the same as I remembered. Dust blanketed everything, thick and untouched, and the only light came from tiny, grimy windows. Rusted medical tools lay scattered across bloodstained tables, and lining the walls were rows of jars filled with murky, yellowed liquid. I couldn't make out what was floating inside, but I knew I didn't want to.

Above me, Manny's laugh echoed, chilling and unhinged. "Oh, you're always at your best when you're angry, Harold."

I forced myself to my feet, the room still spinning. "What the hell is going on?"

Manny ignored me, holding up the locket as it caught the dim light, his eyes gleaming with a manic energy. "What else can I do?" His words were cut short by a wild giggle, his body trembling uncontrollably.

A knot of dread twisted in my gut. "Manny, listen to me. You need to control your breathing. Deep breaths, okay? In and out—"

"Shut up!" He spun toward me, his face contorted in rage, but the erratic twitch in his movements and the barely contained laughter made it impossible for me to feel anything but pity. "Maybe I *want* to lose it. Maybe I'm sick of being a damn hostage! Maybe I want to set this entire place on fire!"

"I understand. Trust me, I've felt the same way. But this won't fix anything."

"Who said anything about fixing it?" Manny barked, pacing wildly. His steps were erratic, his eyes darting around the room like a trapped animal. He kicked over a large metal barrel, and the unmistakable smell flooded the air as the liquid spread across the floor.

The acidic sweetness of it stung my nose, and I gagged, fighting back the nausea that had been clawing at me since this whole nightmare began.

A loud crash echoed through the room, pulling my attention to Manny as he began smashing the jars. The yellow liquid mixed with the clear one, but it was the fleshy mass encased in glass that rooted me in place.

In school, my focus had been on the mind, but that didn't excuse my lack of biology knowledge. I recognized a human heart when I saw one.

My stomach turned violently, and I fought the bile rising in my throat, watching it splatter on the ground near my feet. Another crash rang out, and I couldn't bring myself to look up. I stood there, trembling, visions of autopsy reports flashing through my mind.

"H-Harold?"

I spun to see Abi at the door, his wide eyes darting as if he wished to disappear into the walls. He looked even more ghostly than usual, and when his gaze landed on Manny, who was still lost in his own manic laughter, he let out a small whimper. A part of me longed to scoop him up and flee.

"But that won't help," I murmured to myself. I turned to Abi and forced a smile despite the turmoil inside. "Just wait outside, okay?"

Without waiting for a response, I dashed toward Manny, slipping behind him and seizing his arms. He thrashed against me, but I secured one arm around both his elbows, locking him in place.

Now that he had stopped pacing, it was clear that Manny was far from stable. His body trembled with laughter, and I noticed the tears pooling at the corners of his eyes.

"Breathe, Manny!"

"Fuck you!"

I winced at his anger, knowing I'd have to outlast him. My eyes drifted to the puddle of liquid on the ground. I didn't know what it was, but the sharp, acrid scent told me it wasn't harmless water. Standing in a pool of chemicals surrounded by body parts wouldn't do anything to calm him—and it wasn't safe for either of us.

I glanced at the door. Abi waited on the other side, presumably on the stairs. Taking a struggling man down those steps could easily lead to disaster.

My mind raced for a solution. Based on what Manny had said, the locket had brought us here. If I could somehow retrieve it, maybe—

"I'll kill Emily."

The threat sent a jolt through me, igniting a fire in my veins. I bit down hard on my lip, but Manny's manic laughter was distracting.

"Aww, did that get under your skin?"

My teeth pierced the fresh scabs on my lip, and it became harder to maintain my grip. I wasn't sure if I was losing strength or if Manny had found a sudden surge of power.

"There's no point in beating me up, even if it might feel good to finally let loose, right?"

I inhaled deeply, forcing my thoughts to steady.

"We both know you've figured it out. My little speech only made you feel guilty. Of course, that means you know..."

Maybe hitting Manny wouldn't be entirely pointless—if it could silence him, I might have a clearer shot at controlling the situation.

"A part of you wants to rip her apart. Tear off her arms and legs and—"

I lunged forward, smashing my forehead against the back of his head. Pain shot through me, but it managed to momentarily quiet his voice.

We stood in silence for a moment. Something warm dripped onto my arm, and I realized I wasn't the only one shedding tears. I could feel the laughter had finally stopped.

A hand landed on my shoulder, and I looked up to see Ten beside me. Wordlessly, he moved my hands, freeing Manny and guiding him out of the room. Before they left, Ten glanced back at me. His expression was hard to decipher; he seemed on the verge of tears, yet there was a harshness in his gaze.

Once the door closed, I was left alone in the mess. I should have left, gotten away from the chaos on the floor, but instead, I sank down. The liquid soaked through my pants, but I felt too numb to care.

All I wanted was to disappear.

The door creaked open again, and I looked up to see Abi stepping inside. He stood in front of me, clutching something to his chest. Without a word, he took my wrist and turned my palm upward.

"The greenhouse is still open." Abi placed the locket in my hand and closed my fingers around it. "Or you can leave."

I stared at the locket. My blood still marred its intricate design, but somehow, it felt darker now.

"I don't want to hurt her," I whispered, scanning the now-empty room. I felt hollow, just as I always did after these episodes. "I... I don't."

CHAPTER 10

The Locket's Power

"Come on, Harold! It'll be okay." Emily flashed me a bright smile, though it felt more like a flickering candle in a storm. Today, she'd let her hair cascade free, the sunlight weaving through the golden strands like threads of hope.

She leaned back against the wall, her heels pushing dirt into the tangled tomato vines, their leaves trembling as if sensing the unease in the air. My hands itched to reach for hers, to find comfort in her warmth, but instead, I gripped the edge of my shirt, the fabric rough against my fingers.

"Benten wasn't fond of it." I gripped the fabric of my shirt more tightly, shaking my head as a weight settled heavily in my chest. "I don't want to try it again."

"How are you going to get better if you don't even give it a shot?" Her voice was insistent.

"I can do other things. Making rooms is better. It's... nice. And fun!" The words felt empty as I spoke them, a weak effort to persuade myself.

Without warning, Emily stood up and marched toward the door. "If you won't try, I'm not going to be your friend anymore."

"What?" Panic clawed at me as I forced myself up, my legs feeling like lead. I stumbled after her, but my feet tangled in the gravel, and I fell hard. Pain shot through my knees as the sharp stones bit into my skin, and I couldn't stop the tears from spilling over.

When Emily turned, she gently lifted me, brushing the pebbles off me with a tenderness that felt at odds with my chaos. "Do you think you can get us to the nurse's office?"

With a nod, I raised my hand to my chest. The pendant nestled there felt warm, its presence a familiar anchor. I had never needed to hold it tightly to make it work. I concentrated, picturing the sterile, soft bedding of the nurse's office, filled with the scent of antiseptic and the quiet whispers of comfort. But no matter how desperately I focused, the plants around us remained stubbornly present, their leaves curling in the light.

Emily sighed, her patience wearing thin. "It's okay. I can carry you."

"Oh... okay."

She kneeled, her back a steady support. I stepped forward, ready to climb onto her, when a chilling realization struck. A dampness seeped through my pants. I looked down in horror to see that my pants were soaked, as if I had just sat in a puddle.

"Ewww," Emily wrinkled her nose, her hand instinctively moving to cover it. "What's that smell?"

A slightly sweet yet acidic scent filled the air, cloying and nauseating. My stomach lurched violently. "Emily, I don't feel good."

She turned her head, concern flickering in her eyes as she looked back at me over her shoulder. "Harold?"

I leaned forward, my mouth opening against my will, a soundless cry bubbling to the surface, desperate for a release. As Emily's voice faded, the memory twisted and blurred, pulling me back to the present.

I gagged, but nothing came up. A dull ache throbbed in my knees, yet I pushed through, crawling toward the treatment room's door. The locket pressed tightly into my palm, leaving an indent that reminded me of my urgency. The smell suffocated me. Grabbing the door handle, I pulled myself up and stumbled out of the room.

I shut the door with a forceful bang and collapsed onto the floor. My pants were soaked, and the bandages on my hands weren't faring any better.

"Fuck! Fuck!!" I hissed, tearing at the bandages, desperate to free my hands from whatever they had soaked up.

When I finally pulled them off, I stared in disbelief at my hands. All the cuts had vanished; not even a scab remained. Glancing at the bandages, I noticed fresh smudges of red staining the inside.

I looked back at the door, my mind racing. Had whatever been in the barrel healed my wounds? But if that were true, then why did my knees throb?

Rolling up my pant legs, I found my knees scuffed, bits of stone and dust clinging to the broken skin.

The locket felt heavy in my hand.

I had to find Emily and unravel the mystery of what was happening. I needed to escape this place—burn it to the ground to ensure no one ever returned. The last thing I wanted was to deal with the locket. But despite my efforts, my gaze was drawn to it, unable to look away.

Questions swirled in my mind. I was sure the visions I had were memories. Even though I could recall nothing about the sanatorium, what I had seen felt like a piece of my past. Yet if it were merely a vivid recollection, then my pants wouldn't be wet from the memory, Emily wouldn't have noticed the smell, and the injuries on my hands wouldn't have manifested as bruises on my knees.

A laugh escaped me, tinged with disbelief. I had to figure out if this was truly happening. The problem was that I had no clue how to test it. The memories had surfaced since I'd found the locket, but did they need to center on one? When I explored the first floor, the room had morphed between pristine and ransacked. I hadn't found the locket when everything started shifting, but with how chaotic this place was, could I dismiss the possibility just because I hadn't been holding the damn thing?

I rubbed my face, shaking off the spiraling thoughts. "Get a grip. It might not even be time travel."

But if it was, would it work outside the sanatorium?

Shaking my head, I forced myself to stand. It didn't take long to reach the second floor, once again confronting the same hallway I had first stumbled upon. My gaze fell on the wooden boards laid out near the door closest to me—the spot where the shadowy figure had crouched.

I tightened my grip on the locket and mimicked the motion I had seen. The pendant warmed slightly, and I brought my hand to my mouth to suppress the bile rising within me. But as the feeling subsided, I looked up to find nothing had changed. I was crouched on the floor, alone.

"Does it have to be a memory?" I whispered, my eyes drifting to the spot where I had seen the figure. If it did, then I was stuck with this cursed locket, powerless to use it.

Suddenly, a hand rested on my shoulder, causing me to jump. I turned to see a doctor crouched beside me, his face lined with age and worry, with thinning gray hair and thick glasses that magnified his tired eyes.

The doctor's smile was thin, and his brow furrowed in concern. "Are you alright, sir?"

I hesitated, my mind racing for a response. All I could manage was a nod.

"I see... Well, visitors are supposed to stay with their—" His eyes widened as he scanned the room in a panic. "Sir? Where did—?"

I blinked, and he vanished. The locket burned in my palm, but the nausea that surged through me overshadowed the discomfort. I was going to be sick again. I tried to remember if I'd seen a bathroom anywhere in the maze of rooms, but nothing came to mind. Surely, there had to be a communal one I hadn't stumbled upon yet—but I had no time to waste searching.

I tightened my grip on the locket. Manny had somehow moved us up to different floors; could it take me where I needed to go now?

"Please…" I grunted, feeling heat wash over me. Whether it was the locket's influence or my own body's betrayal, I couldn't tell. All I knew was that I suddenly found myself hunched over an empty toilet.

I didn't know how long I sat there, dry heaving into the bowl, but when it finally stopped, my entire body ached. Shaking, I pushed myself up. The fire in my veins was replaced by an all-consuming chill that made every part of me hurt.

Sitting up, I examined my surroundings. Somehow, I had made it to one of the five stalls. The air was thick with dust, and everything was painted a grim gray, but the black stains smeared against the walls stood out sharply. There were no patterns—no letters or drawings to decipher—just a mess.

Across from me, a long line of hanging sinks revealed pale-orange interiors, their faucets heavily calcified. Above each sink hung small, cracked mirrors, some with chunks missing, reflecting only distorted glimpses of the grim scene.

As I stumbled to one of the sinks, I winced at the sight of my reflection. It was hard to make out many features through the grime, but the few I could see were horrifying. My skin had taken on a sickly green hue, dark bags sagged under my eyes, and my hair was a wild tangle, strands adorned with what looked like grape leaves.

I pulled the leaves from my hair, frowning at their presence. Grape leaves? I didn't remember encountering any vines.

With a frustrated sigh, I dropped the leaves into the sink. "I'm getting tired of this."

My legs wobbled as I made my way out of the bathroom. I found myself on the other side of the second floor, facing a layout that mirrored the one I'd just left. A diagonal hallway led to a room with large windows, while another stretched out in front of me, and a third branched to my left. To my right loomed a second set of spiral stairs.

This was where I'd seen Emily—or at least, what I thought was her. My gaze fell to the locket, still tightly clutched in my fingers. I was sure it had summoned that figure, the one who had whispered to me, kissed me, and insisted I was "perfect" for it.

I recalled feeling queasy then, too. Before I had turned to find Emily standing at the library door, I had been on the verge of vomiting. Each time I experienced these bizarre teleportations or relived memories, nausea clung to me. It had also happened when Manny moved us.

A laugh bubbled up, absurdity washing over me. This whole situation was beyond ridiculous. And Emily somehow was tangled in it all. She knew me as a child—if those memories held any truth— and had lured me here based on the recording and diaries. In the garden memory, she had asked if I could move us to the nurse's office, which meant she had to know about the locket, too.

My stomach twisted as I put the locket back on. "Alright. Here's the deal. You're going to take me to Emily. Not to some magical room or the past or future. You're taking me to my Emily."

After a moment, I felt a gentle pressure on my neck, guiding me toward the windowed room.

"Thank you."

I turned, determination surging as I headed back toward the first floor. I was ready to find Emily and escape this hellish place—if only I wasn't still at the mercy of the damned locket.

CHAPTER 11

A Past Revealed

The locket pulsed with warmth as I neared the windowed room. I blinked, and when my eyes opened again, a spiral staircase had materialized in the center. The pull on the necklace chain stopped, but I no longer needed its guidance. My instincts urged me forward, and I ascended the stairs two at a time, my heart racing in sync with each hurried step.

At the top, there was no door—just an open archway that led into a conservatory bathed in strange, muted light. Stained glass panels lined the walls, connected by twisting green metal frames. The scenes depicted were unsettling—one showed a lavish party in full swing, the next a tiger and donkey in a frantic chase, and another a man raising a cup, vines crawling up his arms. The images felt disjointed and out of place, but there was something vaguely familiar about them.

In the center of the room sat a round, black table with three identical files placed on it. Though the table was large, only two chairs had been set up—plush, deep purple armchairs. The one closest was empty. The other was occupied.

The boy seated across from me looked startlingly like Abi, but his eyes were an unnatural, glowing purple. His face had the softness of youth, yet his expression was sharp, too knowing for someone his age. He leaned forward, smirking.

"Hi, Harold."

"Who are you?" I asked, my heart still hammering.

"You don't recognize yourself?" He tilted his head, his grin stretching wider, stirring an uncomfortable knot in my stomach. "I changed a few things, sure, but it's still me. Definitely better than when I tried looking like Emily."

I pressed my teeth into my lip, trying to regain my composure. "So... you're the locket?"

"If that's what you want to call me." The boy's smirk only deepened. "I can be whatever you need me to be."

"I asked you to take me to Emily," I said, forcing my voice to remain steady.

"I plan to," he replied, his tone deceptively light. "But first, you need to understand who your Emily really is." I clenched my fists, nails digging into my palms. The sensation was grounding, even as the boy let out an amused laugh. "Careful, Harold. I do enjoy a bit of madness, but we don't want to let it out too soon, do we?"

"Just get to the point."

The boy gestured toward the empty chair with a sweep of his hand. With no other options, I sat down. He pushed the three unmarked files toward me, each one identical in its plainness. The boy rested his head in his hands, watching me with unsettling patience.

"Which one do you want to see first?"

I hesitated, then reached for the middle file. The instant my fingers brushed the cover, the conservatory dimmed. The stained glass shifted—the image of the tiger and donkey faded, replaced by a room I recognized right away : the head doctor's office.

The scene was too real, too vivid. Light cream curtains framed the windows, and an older woman sat behind the desk, her blonde hair pulled into a bun. She wore thick gold-framed glasses perched at the end of her nose as she scribbled something on a sheet of paper. To her side, a tape recorder whirred softly, its mechanical buzz filling the silence.

Without glancing up, she spoke, her voice cold and deliberate. "The nurses said you went to see Adelaide."

Though I was watching the memory unfold, I shifted uncomfortably in my chair. My chest tightened as if I were reliving it. The woman's presence felt oppressive and suffocating.

Off-screen, a small, trembling voice replied, "They said she was going to sleep—"

"And they also said you were not to see her," the woman interrupted, her tone sharpening.

"But when Dad went to sleep—"

There was a sudden, violent motion. The woman's hand flew out, and a loud crack echoed through the room. The image jolted, the floor filling my vision, and a stinging sensation flared across my cheek as if I had been struck myself.

I froze, my breath catching. My pulse throbbed painfully in my temples, and my hands gripped the sides of the chair until my knuckles turned white. That dull ache lingered—on my face, in my chest—though I couldn't place why.

"You know the rules."

"But—"

Another hit of pain ran through my ear, and another slapping sound came through the image. After a moment of silence, the woman cleared her throat. "Harold, hand it over."

A shaky set of hands came into view, lifting up a bronze chain. A second later, the locket was placed on the desk. There was the sound of something rolling, and then the woman was raising her hand with a small hammer. The head was only about two inches wide, with one end being flat and the other being rounded. She hovered the hammer over the pendent, and, for a second, I felt my face heat up and my breath quicken.

I wanted to reach through the window, grab the locket, and keep it as far away from the woman as possible. Or, better yet, I could grab the woman and force her away from the desk. From how frail she looked, it wouldn't take long for me to make her regret even thinking about using the hammer. But all I could do was watch as she snapped her wrist. The hammer hit the center of the pendant, and the image went red. A scream echoed around the room, and I felt my throat burn. After a second, I realized that it wasn't just the version of me in the image that was screaming.

The image started to turn back to normal when the woman struck the locket again and again and again. Each time the pain started to fade away, she'd flick her wrist and cause another one. After a while, I found myself face down on the table, my body shaking. Someone was crying, but I couldn't tell if it was from now or from the past.

"You know I don't like doing that—" The sound of something slamming shut echoed around the room, making me wince. "But when you break the rules, I don't have any choice."

"I'm sorry."

"So am I."

The room became brighter, and I was sure that the image of the donkey and tiger was back, but I couldn't bring myself to lift my head yet.

"Are you ready for the next one?"

I did my best to fight back a groan. "What was the point of that?"

"Just like I said, I want what you want. To help you find Emily. Are you ready for the next one?"

The boy pointed toward the last file—the one closest to the image of the man and the cup. I glanced toward the other files, only to find they were gone. I glanced over the back of the chair to find that the archway I'd come in from had been replaced with a stone wall.

"Doesn't seem like I have much of a choice..."

The boy smiled at me.

With a sigh, I reached out and touched the folder. Right away, the lights dimmed again, and the glass window was replaced with a picture of a room I'd never seen before.

The walls and floor were constructed from cold, gray concrete. Candles were set up along a red circle on the ground; the firelight caught against the markings, making it clear that it was freshly painted. Even though I wasn't actually there, I could feel the cold air wrapping around me.

The view shifted downward as the person looked at a large goblet that had been placed on the ground. A small plastic tube was hanging over the rim of the cup with spurts of red liquid pumping out of it in a rhythmic pattern. At the bottom of the cup was the locket; while the liquid was high enough to cover the details and color, it was still possible to make out the general shape.

Distantly, I could make out the sound of chanting. I couldn't understand the words—they weren't in a language that I understood—but something about the sounds was unsettling. I tried to focus on the image instead, only for things to become blurry. My heart rate picked up, pounding desperately in my chest, and I felt sick when the rhythm of the liquid from the tube picked up, too.

"Stop it," I whispered. But the image kept playing.

A low, booming laugh echoed through the chamber, filling the air with a strange, sweet fragrance. The chanting grew louder, more insistent, as whispers joined in, almost like they were brushing against my skin. The room seemed to pulse with each word, but when I glanced around, there was no one else in sight.

Suddenly, warmth spread over me, melting away the tension. A smaller, more childlike laugh bubbled up, blending into the chant. The eerie melody no longer felt threatening—it was almost... inviting. My body relaxed, lulled by the strange harmony.

A pale, delicate hand appeared in the vision, reaching into the crimson liquid inside the goblet. Blood slicked over slender fingers as they pulled out the locket. A shiver ran down my spine as I watched the locket rise, the chain slipping over the person's neck. An unsettling warmth spread through me, and before I knew it, I was giggling softly.

I turned, feeling eyes on me. The boy grinned from across the room, his expression pleased. "Do you remember this?"

I didn't, but somehow, I believed what I was seeing. The terror from the earlier memory and the twisted joy of this one had woven themselves into something undeniable.

The boy's smile faltered as he glanced back at the scene. "Too bad it didn't last long."

The warmth vanished instantly, replaced by the cold, clinical voice of the doctor from the first memory. "Well done, Harold. I always knew you were perfect for this."

A harsh light cut across the floor, casting long, warped shadows as the doctor approached. Her figure loomed over the scene, but the image didn't follow her movements. Instead, a hand entered the frame—long fingers tipped with blood-red nails. She gently took the child's arm, revealing a needle embedded in their vein, attached to the tube draining into the goblet. Efficiently, she removed the needle, carefully bandaging the small wound.

I could almost feel her hand on my shoulder, her nails pressing hard into my skin, sharp enough to leave marks.

"I'm proud of you." Her voice was almost tender, and for a moment, that twisted sense of pride surged through me, washing away the fear. The image finally shifted, revealing her smiling face, warm but predatory.

"I had a thought," she said, her tone dripping with sweet satisfaction. "Since you performed so well today, why don't we have the chefs make something special? I'm thinking... chicken croquettes."

"Really?" The child's voice was filled with fragile hope.

"Really. Everyone will be so happy to hear what you've done for them. Come on now, let's go share the good news."

The lights flickered back on, and the image once again displayed the stained-glass figure of a man holding a cup. I stared blankly ahead, feeling drained and hollow; the fleeting joy ripped away and replaced with an empty void.

When I finally moved, my gaze fell on the last folder. It had returned, sitting quietly, waiting.

"This has nothing to do with Emily," I muttered.

"Not directly," the boy admitted, his voice soft. "But you need to understand."

I slammed my hand against the table. "Understand what? That I went through some messed-up shit as a kid? I *know*. If I didn't, I wouldn't be so angry, so broken. I don't even remember anything before the orphanage. Maybe my brain blocked it for a reason, and I'd prefer to keep it that way rather than let some cursed locket dig it all up!"

The boy's expression softened an apology on his lips. "I'm sorry, Harold."

"Don't." My voice cracked. "Just... don't."

Without another word, the boy climbed onto the table, making his way toward me. He extended his hand and lightly tousled my hair. "I'll let you watch the last memory... whenever you're ready."

I blinked, and when I opened my eyes, the boy was gone. The room was silent, the last file sitting in front of me, daring me to uncover its final, hidden truth.

CHAPTER 12

Emily's Deception

I found myself transfixed by the image in the window, with the last file sprawled across the table before me. The uncertainty of what it might reveal churned a knot in my stomach. If it followed the pattern of the others, Emily likely wouldn't feature at all. Still, I felt an overwhelming urge to escape. But with no other option, I extended my hand and touched the file.

The room darkened once more, and a pungent odor wafted through the air. Music flooded my senses as the scene shifted. Nurses and doctors swirled around the room, caught up in a chaotic celebration of laughter, drinks, and flirtatious exchanges. The view began from the heart of the sanatorium and soon panned toward a staircase.

Just as they were about to slip from the crowd, they turned to the right, revealing a young Emily adorned in a flowing green dress. Delicate fabric leaves framed the hem, and beaded flowers danced along the fabric. A crown of grape leaves rested atop her head, with emerald ribbons woven through her hair.

"Where are you going?" I heard Emily ask.

"I would like to see the others."

She shook her head. "Patients need to rest."

"Then why are we here?"

"Well," Emily hesitated, shifting her weight. "You're the reason we can party. You wouldn't want to be alone, right?"

"No," the boy admitted.

"Then you need your guardian with you." As she spoke, Emily backed up, pulling the image deeper into the swirling celebration.

"Maybe I can leave? Just this once?"

Emily frowned. "No."

"But—"

"I have an idea!" she interrupted. "Why don't you go dance and try having some fun?"

Sitting up straight, my child self responded without hesitation. "Okay."

"Great!" The scene in the window started to spin, showcasing Emily's bright smile at its heart. "You'll be amazing, Harold."

"I will."

Green hues engulfed the scene as my younger self was swept into a hug. "You will! My little god."

The glass panels returned to the window, but I remained unable to tear my gaze away. The boy, or maybe the locket, had compelled me to see these moments of "my Emily," yet she had only been her usual encouraging self this time. It felt as if I was being toyed with for no good reason.

Pushing myself up from the chair, I turned to find the archway I had entered through reappeared. But instead of leading to the stairwell, it now opened into a hidden greenhouse. A part of me wanted to rip the locket from my neck and hurl it across the room, yet I could already sense my body tensing in anticipation of the pain that might follow.

Stepping into the greenhouse, I was met with a disheartening sight: All the plants had wilted. The floor was littered with black, decaying leaves, and the few stems that remained were sickly yellow. When I glanced over my shoulder, I discovered the door had vanished again.

Turning back, I prepared to head toward the desk outside but halted, only steps away from a shadowy figure. Though details were murky, I recognized Emily's silhouette, dressed in a long coat I'd never seen her wear before. She paced the room, scribbling in a journal.

My curiosity piqued, and I leaned in to peer over her shoulder, but the book remained as obscured as she was. I reached out a hand, only for it to pass right through her shoulder. Again, I was left powerless, forced to watch whatever the locket chose to reveal.

Shadow Emily continued her restless pacing for a moment longer before abruptly snapping the book shut and stepping outside. I trailed behind her, the pale-brown grass crunching beneath my feet, each step echoing the desolation surrounding me. The pine trees loomed like blackened sentinels, their needles long fallen, their trunks stark against the ominous gray sky.

I refocused on the image of Emily as she settled at a small table, her hands poised on either side. Instead of pushing them outward as I had, she moved one hand upward and the other downward before vanishing completely.

I blinked at the empty table for a heartbeat, feeling the cold chain of the locket pressing against the back of my neck. It was urging me to replicate her gesture, but would it truly lead to any revelation?

A bitter laugh escaped me. Out of everything happening, questioning this felt absurd.

Sinking to the ground, I placed my hands where Shadow Emily's had been and pushed. The table's halves slid apart effortlessly, revealing a hidden compartment. Inside, a collection of notebooks filled with loose papers was stacked to one side. On the opposite side sat an unfamiliar device—resembling a small television but with a typewriter attached in front, separated by a row of buttons.

As I ran my fingers over the keys, the screen flickered to life, bathing the dim space in a faint green glow.

"Oh," I whispered, realization dawning. "It's a computer."

A cursor blinks in the top left corner, inviting me. I pressed a key, and a letter appeared on the screen. Encouraged, I typed a few more characters until one of my presses caused the cursor to shift lower, and a message materialized:

Error: Passcode incorrect. Please try again.

A thrill shot through me—finally, a sense of control. It wouldn't be easy, but at least I had a clear objective. My gaze darted back to the notebooks; if there was a clue for the passcode hidden within their pages, I had to find it.

Flipping open the first notebook, I recognized Emily's neat handwriting. Each entry followed the same pattern: a date at the top, emotions rated on a scale of one to ten, and a cryptic shorthand comment about someone referred to only as "H." The first two books had detailed daily entries from the past four years, while the subsequent volumes were more sporadic. The last notebook, however, was penned by a different hand, seemingly years older than Emily's first entry.

Piecing it together, "H" had been under observation intermittently for two decades: two entries from the unfamiliar handwriting, followed by an eight-year hiatus, then ten from Emily.

It appeared "H" had struggled with anger as a child, often rated as a seven or nine. Joy was the only other emotion that rivaled it, but even that rarely exceeded five. As "H" matured, the ratings shifted;

they learned to manage their anger, but their emotions fluctuated between joy and fear.

A part of me wanted to challenge the assessments—fear didn't seem right. But admitting that meant confronting who "H" was.

With a chuckle, I closed the books and pushed them aside. "Maybe fear fits, after all."

Turning back to the computer, I surveyed the screen. The notebooks had offered no password hints as I had hoped. Lacking any real understanding of computers, I realized my only option left was to guess the passcode.

My fingers danced hesitantly across the keyboard, my mind racing. Computers were still a novel concept, their inner workings a mystery. The passcode would probably be something recent, a personal secret easily remembered. As my eyes scanned the shadowy corners of the room, a chill ran down my spine. This hidden space felt cloaked in secrecy; had Emily concealed this from the rest of the sanatorium, the passcode would be deeply personal—something tied to her, not to the sanatorium or "H."

My stomach sank as realization dawned: I was grasping at straws. What did I know about Emily? She was relentless about her school-work; her birthday was March 2nd, and she had a penchant for warm meals.

"Is that really all I know about her?" A laugh escaped me, tinged with disbelief. "Four years, and that's it?"

I buried my face in my hands, trying to calm the whirlwind of thoughts. How could I have been so blind to her meticulous notes? Had she been visiting the sanatorium all this time, studying me from the shadows?

I yanked the locket off my neck, holding it up to the flickering screen. "You wanted me to see this, right? Then unlock it."

The screen flickered momentarily, but nothing changed. Instead, the locket began to sway over the keyboard, hovering above a specific key until I pressed it, letting it swing to the next one.

When it finally settled, the word "libertas" materialized on the screen. I hit enter, and the display blinked out for a heartbeat before revealing a flurry of icons. Most resembled sheets of paper, but one in the upper right corner stood out—it was an envelope.

After trial and error, I discovered that one of the buttons acted like a joystick, rolling to guide the pointer on the screen and pressing down to select.

I clicked on the paper icon labeled "1947." It was the lowest of the numbered files. Digital replicas of the entries from the mysterious author filled the screen. Exiting that file, I turned my attention to the envelope icon. Clicking it caused the screen to go blank again before two boxes appeared. The larger box on the right remained empty, but the smaller one on the left displayed various titles from someone referred to only as "The Donor."

Though these messages weren't written in shorthand, they were convoluted and more challenging to decipher than the notebook entries. The brief notes from The Donor expressed gratitude for Emily's updates, but my stomach churned at what I glimpsed in her replies.

Paragraph after paragraph detailed her thoughts on the locket, its purported powers, and the limitations she'd uncovered. Time and again, she emphasized how much more adept "H" was at using the locket. Because of their blood connection, "H" was the only one capable of harnessing its power. She kept repeating that everything would fall into place once she reunited "H" with their rightful place.

A surge of anger surged through me. I thrust my hand through the screen, feeling shards of glass bite into my knuckles as they broke loose, mingling with tangled wires and circuit boards hidden within. Pain radiated through my body, jolting me back as I instinctively recoiled from the sharpness.

I clutched my wrist with my uninjured hand, watching the computer spark ominously.

There was no certainty that any of this was real; maybe it was merely the sanatorium or the locket playing tricks on my mind. But if I found Emily, could I trust her words? What if they were all lies?

I turned and stormed toward the greenhouse. There had to be something in Lyaeus I could rely on—something solid that could tell me the truth about this twisted reality.

If only I could cut through the chaos to uncover it.

CHAPTER 13

The Dark Mastermind

The moment I stepped into the greenhouse, a sudden jolt yanked me out of reality. The air shifted, and I stood in the head doctor's office instead. My eyes widened in disbelief. The shattered window was now pristine, and the desk I had broken stood upright, flawless. The filing cabinet was gone, replaced by a tall bookshelf crammed with medical volumes—some of which I'd studied myself back in school. A chill crept over me as I realized these were the first medical books I had seen in the sanatorium.

Instinctively, I approached the desk. My fingers rummaged through the top drawers, filled with mundane office supplies—pens, pencils, and loose papers. But in the bottom drawer, I hit something more unsettling. Patient files. And sitting next to them, gleaming as if it had never been touched, was a brand new tape recorder. Rows of blank tapes lined up beside it, each with the cryptic label "- IC01" scrawled on the end.

My pulse quickened as I knelt down, feeling for the hidden compartment in the desk—the one where I had found the locket. My fingers grazed the wood until I found a small indent, a clue to the secret within. After several frustrating attempts, I pried the compartment open, nearly ripping my nails. Inside lay two tapes, one marked **S1-04.07.1945-IC** and the other **01S2-04.10.1945-IC01**, and an empty file marked **PN0003021943-03101943** beneath them.

My head spun as I tried to piece together the meaning behind the numbers, but exhaustion overtook me, making it impossible to focus. My body felt like lead.

"Fuck. I'm pathetic," I muttered, slumping into a chair. I attempted a breathing exercise, but it did little to shake the eerie sensation creeping up my spine.

Then, a sharp knock broke the silence. A woman's high, pitched voice followed. "Doctor Collins? May I come in?"

My stomach lurched. Panic surged through me, and I darted into the adjoining bedroom, barely shutting the door without a sound. My heart raced as I crouched behind the door, listening intently. Footsteps approached, then paused, hovering dangerously close to the bedroom. I held my breath, my hand trembling around the S1 tape.

The drawer I'd left open slid shut with a soft whisper. A cold sweat ran down my back—whoever was out there knew someone had been inside. I expected them to come searching any second.

Would the locket save me if they found me? Could it teleport me out of here? Or was I completely at their mercy?

Just as my mind spiraled into frantic possibilities, the sound of the door closing echoed through the room. They had left without even checking for the intruder. I exhaled shakily and rose to my feet, relief mixing with confusion.

The room around me had shifted again. The same orange walls remained, but the details had altered. The once-ornate rug was gone, replaced by plain, bare flooring. The bedding was modest, stripped of any embellishment. A simple desk now stood where the dresser had been, and the shelves were stocked with clothing instead of trinkets.

I walked to the desk, scanning the scattered papers, my eyes locking onto the calendar. April 1944. I gripped the edge of the desk tightly, fighting the dizzying realization. I was standing in a time that preceded my own birth by almost a year. I knew the locket had the power to pull me through different moments in time, but seeing it—feeling it—was something different.

My fingers fumbled through the papers, desperate for an anchor. A small box of envelopes sat in the corner of the desk beside an index card sorter. Each envelope was meticulously labeled with names and addresses. I pulled open the bottom right drawer and found piles of letters—letters from those same addresses. The words within were pleas, each asking about the well-being of a loved one.

My chest tightened. The past was more than a place or time—it was alive, pulsing around me and dragging me deeper into its secrets.

The desk was barren, as though the head doctor had no life beyond his work—no personal touches, no sign of human warmth. It didn't fit with the memory of the lively party I had been shown. Everything felt wrong, sterile.

I was about to inspect the bookshelves when the door creaked open behind me. I spun around, my heart lurching. The doctor—the same one who'd checked on me in the hallway—stood in the doorway, wide-eyed, as if he had stumbled upon something forbidden.

Before I could utter a word, his face grew darker. "Why do you have that?" His voice was a low, accusatory growl.

I glanced down at the tape clutched in my hand and cursed inwardly. "I... found it," I stammered.

He advanced on me, snatching the tape from my grasp. "What do you think you're doing in my sanatorium?" His voice was sharp, laced with authority.

The word "my" made something inside me snap. I bit my lip to keep from shouting, but my body trembled with barely suppressed rage. "*Your* sanatorium?"

His glare intensified, his eyes burning with indignation. "Yes, mine. I've kept order here. I won't let you or anyone else destroy what I've built."

A rush of fury surged through me, unbidden. The memory of my mother's pale, lifeless face flashed before my eyes, followed by the autopsy reports that listed her and my father like cataloged parts. "You're sick," I spat, unable to hold back.

His eyes flashed with something feral, and before I could react, he shoved me back against the desk, his hand clamping around my throat. Panic exploded in my chest, and in that instant, the locket around my neck burned against my skin—a strange, almost other-worldly heat.

His grip faltered, and a low groan escaped his lips. I watched, horri-fied, as his face began to collapse—bit by bit, the skin sloughed off in wet, sickening clumps. His eyes glazed over, liquefying before dripping down his skull. Soon, all that remained was bone, the decayed remnants of a face long lost to time. His hand, once warm, grew cold and stiff, the fingers becoming brittle bones that pressed against my throat.

I staggered backward, heart hammering, as the desk behind me vanished. The room shifted, flickered, and the doctor—if that's what he even was—disappeared as though he'd never been there.

I dropped to the floor, my head falling between my knees as I tried to calm my heaving stomach. My mind was screaming, warning me of something I couldn't comprehend, and my body began to obey. I stumbled out of the bedroom, past the shattered remains of the desk, and toward the front door.

The moment I grasped the door handle, I yanked with all my strength, but the wood didn't budge. Panic clawed at me as I tugged again, harder, but it was as though the door had fused with the frame.

Then I heard it—footsteps approaching from behind. My blood ran cold.

Who was it? Another hallucination? Another trick of the locket? Or was it someone real this time?

Would I have to watch them rot, too?

I released the door handle and clutched the locket tightly, silently begging it to do something—anything. My body tensed, my heart slamming against my ribs as the footsteps grew louder.

Pain surged in my stomach, twisting and gnawing at me, and I barely noticed the dull ache in my head. I shut my eyes tightly, forcing myself to focus on my breathing. The air was sharp and freezing, but it also felt fresh and cleaner than the suffocating atmosphere of the sanatorium. It cut through the haze of panic just enough for me to focus.

When I opened my eyes, everything was different once more.

I was back in the greenhouse, but all the plants were gone. In their place was a vast expanse of snow stretching out as far as I could see. The windows overhead were coated in frost, blocking the light and casting the room into an eerie twilight.

Despite the unnaturalness of it all, I felt an odd sense of relief. The suffocating dread that had plagued me moments ago lifted slightly. Here, at least, I felt like I could hide—from the things chasing me and from the nightmare I couldn't escape.

I collapsed onto a blanket that had appeared on the floor, curling up tightly as exhaustion washed over me. I let my eyes close, surrendering to the quiet. For now, I was safe.

But as soon as my mind drifted, I found myself elsewhere.

I sat at the director's desk, pouring over the stack of receipts documenting the orphanage's purchases over the last decade. Most of the funds went toward food, clothing, and basic supplies, but there were also some suspiciously expensive outings and luxury items mixed in. My frown deepened as I compared my notes to the monthly budget the orphanage was supposed to receive. Something wasn't adding up.

"Director?" I called out, my voice hesitant.

From across the room, the director paused his dusting of the bookshelf and turned toward me. "Is something off?"

"I'm not sure. It's probably my math, but..." I trailed off, unsure how to frame the concern gnawing at me.

He came over and glanced at the paper in front of me. After a brief pause, he nodded. "Your calculations look fine."

I hesitated before saying, "Then we're... We're way in the red."

The director chuckled softly and patted my shoulder. "You're not factoring in the donations."

"Donations?" I frowned. "Did we get that much from donors?"

He gave a small smile, but there was something hollow behind it. "We've been fortunate to receive support from a few... exceptionally generous donors in recent years. They've helped keep us afloat."

I stared at the numbers again. To cover this much of a deficit, the donations had to be substantial—over $5,000, at least. "Do you know who they are? Why they're giving so much?"

The director froze mid-step. When he spoke again, his voice had taken on a strange, tight quality. "No."

"Director?" I pressed, sensing something deeper.

He turned to me, looking older than I'd ever seen him, weariness etched into every line of his face. "Why don't you check on the others? See if they need help with their studies or want to play."

I didn't move. There was no point checking on the other kids. None wanted to be around me. Even after years of therapy, the rumors about my temper still lingered, making me an outcast. That's why I'd ended up here, helping the director with the finances instead of playing with the others.

"If these donors care so much, why don't they just adopt one of us?" I asked, my voice tinged with frustration.

The director sighed heavily, setting the duster down. "Adoption isn't easy. There's a long process—some people just can't get approved."

"Did these donors do something wrong?" I pressed, sensing there was more to the story.

"No," he replied quickly, though his hesitation was clear. Then, with a sharp glance at me, he folded his arms across his chest. "Harold, does the name Evelyn Winters mean anything to you?"

I blink in surprise. "Didn't you ask me that before?"

The director shook his head slowly, his expression troubled. He turned away but didn't resume cleaning. After a long pause, he sighed. "If you ever come across someone named Evelyn Winters... promise me you'll be careful."

My stomach twisted at his words. "Why? What does she want?"

His voice grew tense, almost fearful. "She's been asking about you."

I felt unease. "Do you think—"

"No," he cut me off sharply. "It's not going to happen."

"But—"

"Harold!" His voice snapped like a whip, startling me. His whole body had tensed, and I noticed his knuckles were white from how tightly he was clenching his fists. "Just... forget about this. Please. Go back to your room and focus on your studies."

I opened my mouth to argue but stopped when I saw how badly he was shaking. The director never lost control like this. He was always calm and composed. But now... He looked afraid.

"Okay," I murmured, reluctantly standing up.

"Thank you," he whispered, his voice hollow.

I slipped out of the room, but just before the door closed, I heard a sound that made my blood run cold—the director was sobbing. A part of me wanted to turn back, to demand he tell me what was really going on. But I didn't. Instead, I walked away, doing my best to push Evelyn Winters out of my mind.

As I made my way down the hallway, the echoes of his cries faded behind me, and a heavy weariness settled over my shoulders. The weight of the day faded, and the darkness enveloped me, pulling me deeper into sleep.

CHAPTER 14

Confronting the Hostages

A sharp pain ripped through my abdomen, jolting me awake before I was even fully conscious. I curled inward instinctively, trying to shield myself from the next blow, but it came too fast—Manny's boot connected with my chest, sending a jolt of agony through my ribs.

"Wake up," he barked, his voice harsh and grating.

I let out a groan as he stomped down on my side, the pressure making it impossible to catch my breath. Manny's sneer twisted his features as he leaned over me. "What happened to that fight you showed last time?" His boot lifted again, heading for my face, but this time I was ready. I caught his foot just before it could land, the effort sending a burst of anger surging through me. I twisted hard, and Manny landed on his ass with a satisfying thud.

The urge to pounce on him and let out all my rage was strong, but Abi's wide-eyed stare from across the room made me stop. I forced myself to stand, ignoring the throbbing in my chest, and nodded toward Ten, who sat atop the empty tables. He just glared at me in response, shaking his head slowly.

"So, what now?" Ten asked.

I wanted to answer, but the image of the doctor's rotting body kept flashing in my mind, and the words stuck in my throat. My mouth was dry, the weight of guilt pressing down harder than the pain.

Manny scoffed from the floor, propping himself up on his elbows. "It's obvious, isn't it? You're going to run like a coward. That's what you were planning, wasn't it?"

Abi stepped forward; his voice shaky but defiant. "There's nothing wrong with leaving, Manny! If it keeps him safe—"

"Safe?" Manny spat, climbing to his feet. "He was going to leave us here! Leave us and Emily to rot!"

Ten stood and crossed the room, kneeling to look me dead in the eyes. "You were going to abandon us, weren't you?"

My heart pounded in my chest as their accusations crashed down on me. They weren't wrong. In my desperation, I'd thought about running. About leaving them behind. Even Emily.

Manny leaned closer, his voice dripping with venom. "Does it even matter after everything she's done? Let her burn."

"No," I whispered, my voice barely audible.

Ten shrugged, his expression cold. "You've committed worse acts than leaving someone to die."

"W-what?" I stuttered, but Abi swiftly moved in front of me, arms outstretched, as if he could shield me from their anger.

"Just stop! All of you!" Abi pleaded; his voice desperate.

Manny pushed past him, getting right in my face again. "You think this is over? It's not. Not by a long shot."

I flinched as memories of our last fight flashed through my mind. He'd came at me before, and it hadn't ended well for either of us. But this time, I could see the fire in his eyes—he wasn't done.

"I'm done with this place. Done with all of you!" Manny yelled, slamming his fist against the table, the sound echoing throughout the room.

"But we can't leave!" His voice bounced off the greenhouse walls, drowning out every other sound. The silence that followed was suffocating, broken only by Manny's labored breathing.

I swallowed hard, the tension between us palpable. "How long have you all been stuck here?"

"Twenty-five years for me," Ten said flatly. "Eighteen for Manny. Abi's the newest."

I felt the blood drain from my face. "What the hell..."

Manny's fist slammed down again, cracking the surface of the table. "You don't get to be shocked. You don't get to pretend you care, not when you're the one who gets a way out!"

My pulse raced, anger mixing with fear. I wanted to shout, wanted to fight, but all I could manage was a strained whisper. "What do you want me to do?"

"You figure it out!" Manny yelled, pacing the room in frustration. "You're the one who has to make up for what you did!"

Without thinking, I stood and pulled Manny into a hug. His body tensed, rigid against mine, but I didn't let go. I held him, feeling the weight of his anger, his pain, and his desperation. And in that moment, I knew this wasn't just about surviving anymore. It was about redemption—for all of us.

I threaded my fingers through his hair, trying to ignore the slickness that clung to my hand. He had stopped trembling, and I could feel him begin to unwind. In my mind, I calculated; I must have been nine when he first showed up.

"I'm sorry for shutting you out. I was scared of you and what you made me feel when I was overwhelmed by your presence," I whispered.

"Do you really believe that saying sorry can wipe away all the pain from those years?" he replied, his voice laced with bitterness.

"No, but pretending it never happened won't help either."

He let out a dark chuckle against my shoulder. "I didn't lie. We've been trapped here longer than you think."

It was clear he was trying to provoke me now that I was aware of the truth. I shifted, gently maneuvering Manny toward the blanket, wrapping him up snugly in its warmth. Once I had him settled in the center of the room, Abi draped his arms over Manny's shoulders.

I glanced back to find Ten staring blankly at us. Our eyes met, but his expression was unreadable, still kneeling on the floor. A whirlwind of questions swirled in my mind, and it was obvious Ten was challenging me to voice them.

I turned my attention back to Manny, forcing a smile. "I don't know how to get you out of here or if it's even possible. But if it helps, I could always try setting this place ablaze."

A genuine laugh—far from the manic one he'd had earlier—bubbled up from Manny. "Hell, yes, you will."

I quickly ran through my mental checklist for dealing with anger: using "I" statements, finding something calming, and injecting humor. Each method had offered some relief, yet a dangerous glint still lingered in Manny's eyes.

I was about to guide him through some breathing techniques when he shook his head, sinking down into the blankets. He pulled the edge up to cover himself and Abi. "Forget it. I'm just going to nap."

"If that's what you want," I replied, treading carefully.

He hummed in agreement, settling into the warmth.

After a moment, Abi twisted around to poke his head out from the makeshift cocoon. "Are you planning to leave now?"

"I... I'm not sure."

It took him a moment, but Abi wriggled free from Manny's hold. He crawled over to me, placing his small hands on my shoulders. "You need to run."

A lump formed in my throat. "It's... not that simple."

"Because the door's locked? That's okay! You can just stay here with us forever!"

Ten sighed heavily. "He needs food and water."

"The locket can provide that! And if anything comes up, we can all brainstorm solutions together!"

I stared at him, bemused. The notion of hiding away in the greenhouse for eternity was absurd, but part of me found it oddly alluring. With how bizarre everything was in this sanatorium, was it so far-fetched?

Even without voicing my thoughts, Abi's face lit up, and he wrapped his arms around me. "Thank you!"

For a fleeting moment, I imagined embracing him back. It would be simple to sneak out and grab some vegetables from the second-floor garden to plant seeds of my own. I could spend my days with the three, talking and maybe making things easier for them.

But Ten's glare burned into me, and I didn't need the added pressure to know what my response had to be.

"Abi, we've talked about this."

His grip tightened. "Please, Harold."

"I can't stay." I gently pried his hands off my shoulders and shifted back to meet his gaze. "But I promise, I'll find a way to get out."

Manny sat up, still cocooned in blankets. "Really?"

"I'm furious with Emily; I loathe this place, and... I'm scared. This entire situation terrifies me, and I want to escape as far as I can."

After a beat, Manny chuckled, laying back down. His voice softened with sleep. "Glad you can finally admit it."

I looked at the mound of blankets and frowned. It seemed too small to conceal a person. Just as I had half-expected it, I jumped when I lifted the blanket and found Manny was gone. When I turned back, only Ten remained in the room.

We locked eyes, the tension thick between us.

"You're still here?"

"I'm far from finished with you."

A shiver raced down my spine at the way he said that. As he rose, his form loomed over me, a shadow engulfing my space. I tried to stand, but Ten pressed me back down to my knees. He leaned in, our faces just inches apart, revealing the faint red veins coursing at the edges of his eyes.

"Now that everyone else is out of the picture, I finally have the chance to speak my mind."

"Ten?"

"That feeling in your chest? Tension, they called it." He scoffed, bitterness lacing his words. "But we both know that's far from the truth."

"I have no idea what you mean."

"No, you don't."

With that, Ten stepped back, pacing toward the greenhouse exit, staring into the expanse of white that lay beyond. His silhouette appeared small against the vast field, and for a fleeting moment, I felt like an intruder in his world. But when he turned back, I was taken aback by the tears streaming down his face.

"Benet, Kantos, Daniel, Philip, Gail, Penny, Karl, Hazel, Kim, Wallace, Pachi, Hugo, Kay. Do any of them resonate with you?"

I wanted to deny it, but the truth was clear. "I'm sorry."

"It's fine," he chuckled softly, a humorless sound that made his entire figure slump. "It's always been my duty."

I scrutinized his words, confusion swirling in my mind. "What do you want from me?"

Ten shrugged. "You told Abi you were leaving."

"But—"

"Don't. Just... leave. It's probably for the best."

My heart ached, a pang of guilt swelling within me. I longed to do something for him, just as I had for the others, but I couldn't even recall what I'd done for them.

After a moment of hesitation, I brushed past Ten, heading toward the table. The snow clung to my legs, sending icy tendrils of discomfort shooting up my body. I crouched by the table, shaking off the chill as I focused on my task. I swept my hand across the surface, clearing it as best as I could, then pried open the edges to reveal the contents beneath.

There, amid the scattered diaries and letters I had discovered on my previous visit, I finally spotted a blank sheet at the back of one book. I ripped it free and hurried back to Ten.

"Do you have something to write with?"

He raised his empty hand, forming a fist. A tight knot formed in my stomach, but when he opened it, a red crayon rested on his palm.

I hurriedly wrote down each name, a strange familiarity nagging at me as I penned them. After folding the note, I tucked it into my pocket.

"I'll memorize them each night. I don't know if it will make a difference, but..."

Ten nodded solemnly. "Goodbye, Harold."

For a moment, I hesitated, unsure how to respond. Before I could gather my thoughts, he turned away and began marching through the snow.

Stepping out of the greenhouse, I found myself in the dimly lit hallway of the second floor of the sanatorium. The door creaked shut behind me, and I exhaled shakily. The thought of removing the locket and escaping through the window I had entered crossed my mind.

But as soon as that idea took root, I crumpled to the floor, clutching my neck as searing pain radiated through me. The locket burned against my skin, an unyielding grip that kept it fastened.

All I could do was endure the fiery agony spreading through my body, threatening to consume me whole.

CHAPTER 15

The Breaking Point

Heat radiated from the chain of the locket as my fingers grazed it, yet I couldn't seem to grasp it. The necklace remained stubbornly in place, and despite the flexibility of my fingers, every attempt to encircle it was met with failure. All I could do was curl up on the cold ground, hoping this torment would soon subside.

The sound of footsteps echoed through the emptiness, gradually drawing closer. A gentle hand began to run through my hair, soothingly trailing down my back in comforting circles. As the warmth spread through me, I felt the pain gradually fading away.

When I opened my eyes—though I hadn't realized they were shut—I was met with my reflection hovering above me. The only difference was the shimmering purple eyes and a delicate crown of leaves woven into the hair of this illusion. I should have pushed it away, but desperation for comfort held me captive.

I let my head sink into the illusion's lap, feeling the locket's warmth change; it was still there, but the burning had dulled to a gentle heat.

"How are you?" the illusion asked, its voice smooth like honey.

I hummed softly. "Better."

"Good." The hand moved to massage my temples, the pressure soothing my frayed nerves. "Are you ready?"

"Soon."

The image nodded, a knowing look in its eyes. "Just let me know when you are ready... Then we can leave."

My stomach twisted with unease. "What?"

He arched an eyebrow and repeated the words slowly as if to emphasize them. "Then we can leave."

Sitting up, the world around me swirled, and for a moment, darkness enveloped my vision, dizziness sweeping through me. When I blinked back clarity, the illusion's face was unnervingly close, a smirk playing on its lips.

"Feeling better?"

My heart raced in my chest. "What do you mean by 'leave'? Where are we going?"

"I've made plans," he replied, brushing my hair behind my ear with a feather-light touch. "There are things I need to show you."

Panic surged within me, and I instinctively tried to pull away, but the illusion gripped my shoulder, anchoring me in place. "Are you ready?"

Before I could respond, the familiar pain returned, sharp and insistent. My body crumpled to the ground, the comforting presence of the illusion vanishing like smoke. The hallway melted away, replaced by an abyss of darkness. Even seated, I felt suspended in nothingness, the ground beneath me gone.

"Stop it," I whispered, though the words barely escaped my lips, swallowed by the void.

Shivers coursed through me. I should have left ages ago. I shouldn't have allowed myself to be caught in this web of deceit. Why had I let this happen for so long?

As if summoned by my despair, a cascade of colors exploded before me. It took a moment for me to register what I was seeing —the lush green of the campus stretched out beneath a brilliant sky. The voices of students mingled in the air, vibrant and alive.

A warm hand rested on my back, and I turned to find Emily standing there, her form exactly as I remembered from my second year and her first year. The setting sun caught the loose strands of hair escaping her braid, illuminating her gray eyes with a captivating shimmer. My breath hitched in my throat, just as it always did in her presence. She was breathtakingly beautiful, and every time I saw her, the feeling was as intoxicating as the first.

Emily settled beside me with a smile. "This is why."

"What do you mean?"

Her laughter rang out, but it was a wild sound that sent shivers down my spine. In an instant, I found myself shoved onto a bed that had appeared out of nowhere. The dimness of the room engulfed me, the details swallowed by Emily's face as she leaned in for a kiss.

Her lips were icy against mine—my instincts kicked in, and I knew this was an illusion. I grasped her shoulders, pushing her away, but she effortlessly repositioned herself, now sitting on my stomach with a predatory grin.

"You love her." She leaned in, her breath warm against my ear as she seductively whispered, "But she doesn't feel the same way about you."

A wave of cold dread washed over me, and I shoved her away with all my strength. As I sat up, light flooded in from a window that hadn't existed moments before. Sitting on the floor, a younger version of Emily gazed up at me—not the figure who had just been on top of me, but Emily as a child, her hands covered in bright red blood that dripped from a bizarre cat drawing beneath her. Her impossibly wide smile made my stomach churn.

I staggered, my legs feeling oddly short and unsteady, but I rushed out of the room. The hallways were bright and pristine, yet strange symbols adorned the walls, their meanings slipping from my grasp as I dashed past. Without thinking, I slammed my hand against a nearby door.

As the door swung open, I instantly recognized the old woman within. "Ms. Pachi," I breathed.

"Ah, Harold," she said, a hint of surprise in her voice. "I wasn't anticipating your arrival for another few hours."

My heart raced, confusion clouding my mind as I tried to retreat, but my feet felt glued to the floor. The weight of the locket around my neck pulled at me.

Suddenly, everything around me began to dissolve once again. The world blurred and shifted, colors melting together until I was thrown back into the hallways of the sanatorium.

Panic seized my chest as I tore down the corridor, each step a desperate attempt to outrun the suffocating madness closing in around me. My breath came in ragged gasps, sharp and uneven. The air felt thick, suffused with whispers that slithered through the walls, warping reality and twisting my thoughts into knots of terror. I ran, not because I knew where I was going, but because standing still meant surrendering to the madness, the darkness that had wrapped itself around me since the moment I stepped into this cursed place.

The laughter echoed in my ears—a mocking, cruel sound that pulled me back into the past, to the shadowed corners of my child-hood. It was the laughter of torment, the jeering taunts of control, reminding me of what I had once been: a puppet of fear, twisted by obedience, marionetted by unseen hands.

Suddenly, in the flickering light of a doorway, she appeared. A young Emily stood there, no older than she had been when I first met her. Her eyes gleamed, dark pools reflecting an innocence long gone, tainted by something far more sinister. She tilted her head, her smile unnervingly wide, a grotesque parody of joy. "Pain is good," she sang, her voice disturbingly bright, as if she were playing a cruel game. "Remember what I told you, Harold? Pain is the only way to feel alive."

I opened my mouth to scream, to protest, but no sound came out. My throat tightened as memories swirled around me, suffocating me in a flood of past horrors. "You deserve this, Harold," her voice taunted, now echoing from all directions as if the walls themselves were speaking. "It makes you strong. The pain... It's what keeps you alive. Without it, you're nothing."

I stumbled forward, my legs weak, the corridor warping around me, its walls pulsing with whispers and screams. The guttural cries of patients pierced the air—too close, too real—agonized, as if they were trapped somewhere between this world and another. Surgical drills whined in the distance, the sickening grind of saws slicing through bone mingling with the agonizing crunch of cartilage. The sounds weren't just noise—they were memories clawing at me, dragging me back into the rituals, the blindfolds, the chanting that had haunted my past.

A sudden click. A hiss. The sound of a tape recorder snapped to life, and a cold, clinical voice cut through the chaos like a blade. "Harold," the head doctor's voice oozed with calm authority, his tone hypnotic, unnerving. "Tell me about the locket. What does it mean to you?"

I faltered, my legs buckling beneath me. The voice was everywhere —above me, beneath me, inside me. "Does it remind you of the pain you've caused?" The question echoed, and the walls seemed to close in around me. "Does it make you feel powerful?"

Each word slashed through me, cutting deeper than any blade. Faces flashed before my eyes—contorted in agony, twisted by fear.

Their pain was my doing. I could hear chants beckoning me to give in, embrace the chaos, and let it consume me whole. "You need to release it, Harold," Emily's voice whispered in my ear, close enough I could feel her breath. "This pain... It's the only way."

The doctor's voice interwove with hers, cold and unrelenting. "Remember, the locket is your key, your guide. It gives you what you need, Harold. Everything that has happened—it's what you wanted, isn't it? You crave the chaos. You thrive on it. It's who you are."

I shook my head violently, trying to rid myself of the voices, but they clung to me like shadows, creeping into every corner of my mind. "You've always been drawn to the locket," the doctor continued, his voice sharp, almost gleeful. "It's your power, Harold. Your strength. Can't you feel it? It's not a burden—it's your gift."

The world around me warped and shifted. The walls bent, the floors twisted, and I was sinking into something dark, something far beyond my control.

Images of the past flashed before my eyes—rituals that twisted innocence into something grotesque. I could still feel the weight of the blindfolds, the chanting of a cult as they stripped away any shred of humanity I had left. The doctor's voice slithered through my mind, relentless. "You wanted power, Harold," he pressed, his words like a scalpel cutting through my resolve. "The pain they inflicted on you —you had the power to break them. You chose this. You embraced the suffering because it made you feel alive."

My feet stumbled, dragging me into another room, where grown Emily stood waiting. She wasn't the girl from my memories anymore. She was something darker, something far more dangerous. Her presence pulled me in, magnetic and suffocating, her eyes gleaming with a predatory intensity. She stepped closer, her voice low and sultry, like a siren beckoning me to my doom. "You don't have to be afraid, Harold." Her lips curled into a smile, mocking but hypnotic. "Just give in. Let it take you. It's what you deserve."

A sickening wave of fear surged through me; the instinct to flee was overwhelming. "No!" I shouted, spinning on my heel to escape, but her laughter echoed, sinister and close, following me like a shadow. No matter where I turned, she was always just behind me, her presence unavoidable.

I staggered forward, trying to shake off her influence, but the doctor's voice wormed its way back in, calm and authoritative. "Every decision you made, every ounce of pain you caused—it was always your choice, Harold. The locket is your ally, your key to control. Accept it, and you'll find clarity."

Each word sliced deeper, twisting in my mind like a jagged blade. Memories surged, flooding my thoughts—patients in the sanatorium, their eyes wide with terror, mouths gagged, forced to endure the twisted teachings of this cursed place. Their screams clawed at me, filling the halls with a relentless chorus of agony.

Emily's image flickered before me, her face shifting between the girl I once knew and the woman she had become. Her eyes gleamed with that same knowing intensity as if she held the answers I was too terrified to confront. "Deep down, you know you can't escape it, Harold," she whispered. "This place, our past... It's calling to you. I wanted you to remember. You were always meant to come back."

The hallway stretched endlessly before me, the walls warping and shifting, twisting into something unnatural. It was as if I were being swallowed by the building itself, trapped in an eternal loop of terror and torment. My past and present collided, blurring the lines between the scared child I had once been and the broken man I had become.

But it wasn't just the sanatorium that wanted me—it was Emily. She wanted to control me, to pull me deeper into this madness. But why? What did she want from me? The questions gnawed at my mind, but one thing was clear: She wasn't just here to haunt me. She had a purpose, and I needed to uncover it before it consumed me completely.

I came to a halt, my breath ragged, my heart pounding in my chest. I couldn't keep running. If I did, I would lose myself to the madness forever. No more avoiding the inevitable. If Emily wanted me to confront this, I would face it head-on. I wasn't here to save her anymore. I was here for answers—for the truth, no matter how twisted it might be.

Suddenly, everything around me fell into an eerie silence, the oppressive weight of the sanatorium bearing down on me like a suffocating fog. The whispers, the screams, the doctor's voice—they all vanished, leaving only a cold, dreadful quiet. I stood before a door—the heart of this cursed place. My skin prickled, an icy chill crawling down my spine as I stared at it, knowing, without understanding why, that something was waiting for me behind that door.

I reached out with trembling hands. The doorknob was cold against my skin, the metal biting into my flesh as I gripped it tightly. I hesitated for a moment, my breath shallow, my heart pounding in my ears. Something was on the other side, something I couldn't fully comprehend—but I knew, deep down, that it was waiting for me.

CHAPTER 16
The Final Illusion

I entered the room, my heart pounding in sync with the oppressive energy in the air. The darkness was alive—a roiling mass of dark red smoke twisting and curling like tendrils from a smoldering flame. Half-formed faces floated just out of reach, their mouths moving in silence as if trapped between worlds. They licked at my mind, tugging at old wounds, pulling me deeper into the smoke until it felt like I was suffocating under the weight of my past.

And in the middle of it all stood Emily.

She was so still, so impossibly calm—the red smoke parted for her. Her face was exactly as I remembered: soft, gentle, full of that warmth that had always drawn me in. For a moment, I wanted to believe she was real. Maybe, just maybe, she was here to save me from this nightmare.

But something was wrong.

Her stillness wasn't peace—it was too perfect, too deliberate. And her smile. There was something off about it. Too knowing.

"Harold," she said softly, her voice cutting through the noise around us. "You came back to me."

I froze, my feet rooted to the spot. I wanted to go to her, to fall into the comfort of her arms like I used to when things got too heavy. But something inside me resisted. My Emily wasn't here—she was out there, far away from this nightmare.

"Emily..." I breathed her name. But I knew better. This wasn't her. This twisted version of her was nothing more than a manifestation —the locket's grip on me, twisting guilt and regret into something tangible.

Her smile widened, but it wasn't the smile that used to light up her face. It was something darker. "You've been fighting this for too long, Harold." Her voice was smooth and familiar, as though she was slipping into old rhythms, the way she used to when we'd talk late into the night. "The locket... It's not something you can run from."

I shook my head, stepping back slightly. "Emily, this isn't real."

Her eyes flickered—just for a moment, something sharp flashing in them. "Real? Harold, don't you see? I've always been real. I've always been here. You've held on to me for so long; I'm part of you."

There it was—that familiar cadence, the way she used to speak when she wanted to convince me of something. The way she'd tug at my stubbornness, making me see her side. I used to love that about her. But now... Now, it felt wrong. Manipulative.

She stepped closer, her voice dropping to a whisper, "You think you can just walk away? After everything? After all we shared?" Her fingers lightly grazed my arm, and for a split second, it felt real—just like before. "You said you'd never leave me, Harold. That you couldn't live without me. And yet, here you are. Running."

Her smile grew softer, and she tilted her head like she used to, back when we'd talk for hours about things that never mattered. "You don't need to run anymore. You've carried this for so long... don't you see? You've been keeping the truth from yourself."

The truth. The word echoed in my mind, rattling loose fragments of memories I couldn't place. "I don't know what you mean," I said, shaking my head. "This isn't real. You're not real."

Her eyes flashed with something—disappointment, maybe. Hurt. But it didn't feel like Emily. "You *do* know, Harold. You've always known. That locket..." Her gaze flicked toward it, the metal now burning cold against my chest. "It's part of you. You've carried it for so long; you just forgot."

I glanced down at the locket, my fingers instinctively wrapping around it. It felt heavy—far heavier than it should have. I didn't remember when I first put it on. I don't remember *why* I had it at all. "I don't..." The words stuck in my throat, confusion choking me.

Her voice softened, coaxing me the way she used to when she wanted me to open up. "You've suppressed so much, Harold. But you don't have to fight it anymore. You *gave in* once... you can do it again."

I froze, the blood draining from my face. *I gave in?* What did that mean? My mind raced, trying to recall—flashes of the past came in jagged fragments: shadows, whispers, the cold weight of the locket. But nothing concrete. Nothing that made sense.

"No," I muttered, backing away slightly.

Her voice cut me off, sharper now. "You can't keep running from this. From what's inside you. You think you can just ignore it? Forget everything that happened? *We* happened, Harold."

I flinched. The words hit harder than I expected, twisting something in my chest. But I shook my head. "No, *you're not her.* Emily wouldn't do this."

I met her gaze, my breath shallow, forcing myself to hold steady. "You're not real," I whispered, my voice shaking but defiant. "You're just a ghost."

Her face twisted with fury, her calm veneer cracking. "You don't get to walk away!" she hissed. "You *need* the locket. You *need* me."

The words hit me, sharp and painful, but I didn't flinch. Not this time. "No," I said, standing taller, voice firm. "I'm done. With the locket, the guilt—*you*. You don't control me anymore."

Her form flickered, red smoke curling and tightening around her, her expression warping into rage. With a final scream, a banshee-like wail that ripped through the room, her figure shattered. Shadows lashed out, the smoke thickening, swirling in a violent storm of memories and darkness.

But as her form dissolved into the chaos, I wasn't free. The smoke didn't dissipate—it thickened, turning suffocating. Memories buried for years—locked away—rose to the surface like poison breaking through the skin.

And it all started with the locket.

Suddenly, I was back—a younger version of me, hunched on the edge of a cold cot in the sanatorium. The air was heavy with the stench of dampness and fear, the walls closing in like a tomb. The locket dangled from my neck; its weight unbearable. I didn't understand it then—how it wasn't just an object. It was a conduit for something far worse. Something cursed.

Emily was there, too, sitting across from me. Her voice was low and coaxing like it always had been. "Just listen, Harold. Do what they ask, and it'll be over soon. The experiments... the pain... It'll stop. We can leave this place behind."

I looked into her eyes, searching for reassurance. But behind that calm façade, there was fear—a fear she hid from me, a fear she knew all too well. She had lied. The pain didn't stop. It grew.

Dr. Winters. That name still made my skin crawl. Her cold, clinical voice echoed through my mind as the scene twisted, pulling me deeper into the memories. She had been the one in charge—the mastermind who pulled the strings of our torment.

I could see her now, standing over me during one of the endless "sessions." Her voice was sharp and calculated. "Inflict the pain, Harold. You can't avoid it. It's part of the process."

I didn't want to. I resisted. I hesitated.

And then she turned to Emily.

I had forgotten this—buried it so deep I thought I'd never have to relive it. But there she was. Emily, strapped to the chair, her usual composure breaking, her breath hitching as she stared at the instruments laid out before her. Dr. Winters' tools of torment.

The tension in Emily's body grew, her eyes darting between the doctor and me. Her promises, her calm assurances—that it would all stop—were lies. And now she would pay for them.

I saw everything.

The sharp screech of metal as Dr. Winters lifted one of the tools, holding it just long enough for Emily to see what was coming. Emily's knuckles turned white against the leather straps. Then, the sharp, unmistakable sound of flesh tearing—her body jerking violently as the instruments sank into her.

Her screams.

They echoed in my mind, tearing through my sanity. The agony in her voice, the way her body convulsed under the force of the pain— it was too much. It was inhumane.

But I couldn't look away. Dr. Winters made sure of that. She forced me to watch as she cut deeper, the metal glinting with blood, her hands working with precise cruelty. Every scream and every jolt of pain from Emily's body was like a hammer blow to my psyche.

Even then, even through the horror, Emily whispered, her voice cracking with pain. "This... pain... means you're alive, Harold. It's... a blessing." Her voice faltered, strained. "You have to... accept it... give it... to others..."

Her words twisted inside me, filling me with an indescribable dread. She had bought into it. Into Dr. Winters' lies. She believed it. Or maybe she just needed to, to survive. But I couldn't accept it. I couldn't believe it.

The memories shifted violently, swirling into focus like a dark, turbulent storm I could no longer suppress. The image of Emily blurred; her face still contorted with anger, but her form began to distort, fragmenting as the truth rushed in.

I had induced the pain.

My heart raced, the room spinning around me as the illusion peeled away, replaced by memories far worse than anything I'd tried to bury. I was back in a chamber where the sickening rituals took place —where I had crossed the line.

Emily had always been there, whispering promises of escape, false hope that kept me tethered. But it was Dr. Winters who had pushed me over the edge. *She* had been the mastermind, orchestrating every twisted step of my descent. The locket—a cursed object of power— had latched onto me, and I had let it happen.

The chamber was cold, lit only by the dim, flickering candles. I remembered standing in front of Ms. Pachi—her hands tied to the altar, her wide, terrified eyes fixed on me. My hand trembled as I held the blade, the weight of the locket at my chest, urging me forward.

I hadn't wanted to do it.

But the locket... **It demanded blood**.

The chanting filled the room, the members watching with hollow, expectant eyes. Dr. Winters had instructed me precisely how deep to cut and how much blood would be enough to satiate the locket's hunger. Ms. Pachi's voice quivered in prayer, her pleas falling on deaf ears. There was no mercy here. Not for her. Not for me.

I pressed the blade to her forearm, as instructed, feeling the gush of blood as it began to flow. The locket thrummed against my skin, feeding on her agony. Her cries echoed in the room, but the chanting only grew louder, a twisted symphony urging me to continue.

But it wasn't enough. The locket demanded **more**.

I lifted the blade higher, my own heart hammering against my chest, my hand shaking as I positioned it above her heart. Ms. Pachi sobbed, her body writhing in terror, but I was already too far gone. The locket tightened its grip on me, clouding my mind.

The blade plunged down.

Her scream shattered the air, a wail so piercing it seemed to shake the ground. Blood gushed from the wound, spilling onto my hands and staining my skin. The locket pulsed brighter, drinking in her life force, its power filling the room with a dark, suffocating presence.

I watched as her body convulsed, the life slipping from her with every beat of her heart, until finally, she went still.

In the aftermath, I stood there, numb, staring at her lifeless body. The silence was deafening. The chanting had stopped. The locket, glowing fiercely around my neck, was quiet now, satisfied. But inside me, something had broken. I had crossed a line I could never uncross. And what enraged me most wasn't just that I had done it— it was that **I had reveled in it.**

That was when I knew the locket wasn't just an object—it was my master. I was no longer Harold. I was a monster shaped by the locket's cursed power.

As the memory dragged me deeper into its grasp, suffocating me in its darkness, another face appeared—my mother. Her image flickered like a dying flame, her face twisted with sorrow and desperation.

"Stop, Harold. Stop this madness," she had begged, her voice trembling with fear.

But I couldn't. The locket's hold on me was too strong, its power seeping into every corner of my mind, erasing the line between who I had been and who I had become.

I was slipping into madness, and I had let it happen.

The room seemed to close in on me, the air thick with the weight of everything I had done. I could feel the locket burning against my chest, binding me to the horrors of my past.

And then, amid the suffocating silence, a slow, deliberate clap echoed behind me.

Clap. Clap. Clap.

The sound cut through the darkness like a knife, sharp and mocking. Every muscle in my body tensed; my breath caught in my throat. I didn't need to turn around to know someone was there.

"Harold," a low, familiar voice purred. "It's been some time."

My heart lurched in my chest. I knew that voice—its smooth, menacing tone was burned into my memory. Fear surged through me, sharp and unrelenting, as I tried to place it, but my mind scrambled, the answer slipping through my fingers.

I slowly turned, my body trembling as the shadows thickened around me. And there, looming in the dim light, was the figure I had feared for so long.

The figure from my nightmares.

CHAPTER 17

The Puppet Master Revealed

The figure stepped into the light, and recognition slammed into me like a physical blow. **Dr. Evelyn Winters**. I knew her. Her sharp cheekbones, the piercing eyes, and the way her gray hair framed her face—she hadn't aged much. The memories were returning faster now—images of her guiding those experiments, her voice whispering twisted promises in the dark. A shiver crawled up my spine.

I wasn't just remembering her; I feared her.

"Harold," she purred, her voice cold yet seductive, dripping with authority. "It's been too long."

My heart raced, dread swelling inside me. The experiments. The rituals. The teachings. Everything about her felt wrong, and yet something in me knew this fear wasn't just born from memory. It was deeper than that, primal.

"What do you want?" I croaked, my throat tight. I had to fight to keep my voice steady.

Evelyn's smile widened into a serpentine grin. "Oh, Harold," she cooed. "This has never been about what I want. It's always been about *you*."

I stepped back, recoiling at the weight of her words. "I don't understand," I said, though a part of me dreaded the answer.

"You've never fully understood, have you?" she continued, stepping forward, her eyes gleaming with the same unsettling delight they always had. "From the very beginning, you were never just another subject in our trials. You were destined for far more. You're *special*, Harold. Chosen. The heart of the awakening."

"Chosen?" The word tasted bitter in my mouth. "For what?"

"To serve Dionysus," she said, her voice reverent now, as though the name held divine power. "Not a god of chaos, as so many would believe, but a liberator. A force beyond this world, one that can bring true equality, true freedom. And you—*you* are the key to his return."

I stared at her, confusion swirling in my mind. "What does Dionysus have to do with me? Why me?"

Evelyn's eyes darkened, her voice growing low and intense. "You've been touched by Dionysus since the day you were born, Harold. The locket—an ancient relic gifted to us by his followers—was drawn to you. Only you could wield its power and unlock its true potential."

I felt the weight of the locket against my chest, cold and oppressive. "I didn't choose this," I whispered, my voice cracking.

"But it chose you," she replied, her tone almost tender. "The locket has bound itself to you, Harold. You are the chosen vessel through which Dionysus will return. It's why you survived the rituals as a child. Why you've always felt its pull. The suffering, the power—it all leads back to him. You've felt it, haven't you?"

My breath caught in my throat. She was right. The locket had always felt like more than just an object. Its energy coursed through me, feeding off the pain and fear it demanded, pushing me toward something darker, something inevitable.

"I won't let you control me," I said, though my voice shook. "I'm not your puppet."

Evelyn's smile twisted into something more sinister. "Oh, Harold," she said softly. "You've never been in control. Even your precious Emily—do you really think she was just an innocent bystander?"

My chest tightened at the mention of Emily's name. "What about her?" I asked, the dread creeping into my voice.

"Emily," Evelyn said, her eyes narrowing, "is my daughter. She was always part of the plan. She was never just someone you happened to meet. She was placed in your life—by me. Everything she did was to prepare you, to shape you into the vessel you were meant to be."

Evelyn's gaze hardened, a flicker of annoyance crossing her face. "Honestly, I wish it had been Emily who was chosen," she continued, her voice sharp. "She's always been so much easier to work with than you—obedient, focused, and far less... *complicated*. But no, it had to be *you*. Dionysus chose *you*." She spat the last word with thinly veiled frustration.

"No," I whispered, shaking my head.

Evelyn's laughter echoed in the room, cold and sharp. "Yes, Emily cared about you, but it was always part of a bigger plan. Through her, I could guide you without you even realizing it. Every step you've taken has brought you to this moment."

My mind reeled, trying to process the weight of her words. Emily— manipulating me? Could that really be true?

"Why me?" I choked out. "Why am I so important to all of this?"

Evelyn's expression softened, though her eyes burned with a manic intensity. "Because Dionysus is a god who thrives on human extremes—pain, joy, fear, ecstasy. Only someone who has experienced it all, who has been broken and rebuilt by the locket, could ever summon his true power. You, Harold, are that person. The perfect vessel. Your suffering has prepared you for this."

I staggered back, the weight of her words crashing down on me. The locket pulsed against my chest, a dark, insistent reminder of the power it held over me.

"You can fight it," she said, stepping forward. "Or you can embrace it. Dionysus will return, and through him, we will remake the world. No more suffering, no more inequality—everyone will be free."

Her voice dropped to a whisper; her eyes gleaming with fanatical fervor. "And you, Harold, will stand at his side as the one who brought him back."

"I won't let you use me," I said, though the certainty in my voice faltered.

"You don't have a choice," Evelyn said simply. "Dionysus has chosen you, just as the locket did. You're bound to him, Harold. Whether you like it or not."

The air around us seemed to thicken, the darkness pressing in. I felt the locket's pull growing stronger, feeding off my fear and my confusion. I didn't know how to fight it; I didn't know if I could.

And deep down, a terrifying thought gnawed at me: *What if she was right?*

The smoke thickened around us, memories spiraling in the crimson haze, twisting into grotesque reflections of the past I had once clung to. In the swirling fog, I caught glimpses—*real* memories—of Emily and me as children, huddled together in the darkness.

"We'll get out of here, Harold," Emily had whispered, her small hand gripping mine tightly. Her eyes, wide with fear but filled with determination, locked on mine as we hid from Evelyn's cruel gaze. "We'll escape one day. I promise."

The scene shifted, distorting, but that promise—*her* promise— echoed in my mind.

My hands shook, the depth of Evelyn's manipulation crashing down on me. "Emily would never help you," I choked out, my voice filled with disbelief. "She wanted to escape. She wanted to save us both."

"Did she?" Evelyn's laughter echoed, cold and mocking. "Or was she simply doing what she was trained to do? She believed in the cause, Harold. Just as you will. I made her strong—just as I will make you. Together, we can fulfill the will of Dionysus."

I flinched at the mention of that name. "Dionysus? You mean chaos—madness! You think this is some divine purpose? This is insanity!"

Evelyn's smile widened; her eyes alight with a twisted fervor. "Oh, but that's the beauty of it. Dionysus feeds on the pain and chaos of humanity. Through suffering, we can transcend. The weak aren't meant to be protected, Harold; they're meant to be sacrificed. Only those who endure the agony and embrace their true nature will rise above the rest."

I recoiled at her words, bile rising in my throat. "You're talking about tyranny and slaughter! That's your vision?"

"Not tyranny—*ascension*," she corrected, her voice dripping with zeal. "I will guide this broken world into a new era, where the chosen few—the strong—flourish while the weak feed the power of the divine. And you, Harold, are at the center of it all."

"By using me? By controlling me?" I shouted, my voice raw with anger. "You're a monster, not a savior!"

Evelyn's eyes darkened. "Dionysus chose you for a reason. You are the key to unlocking his power, the vessel through which we will bring the world to its knees. Your suffering has only strengthened you—your fear, your anger—all of it feeds him. Embrace it, and you will know true strength."

"I'll never help you," I snarled, my voice trembling with defiance.

Her expression hardened, fury sparking in her eyes. "You will, Harold. Whether you like it or not. You belong to Dionysus now. If you resist, you will suffer even more—but you can choose to be part of something far greater."

"I'd rather die than be your pawn," I spat.

Evelyn leaned closer; her voice soft but dripping with venom. "You've always belonged to me, Harold. You were created for this. And soon, you will see that you have no choice."

Suddenly, she reached into her pocket and produced a small vial filled with a dark, viscous liquid. "This will help you understand your true purpose," she said, her voice low and sinister. "Just a single drop, and you'll be flexible—prepared to accept your true self."

I lunged at her, but she was quicker. The vial uncorked with a soft hiss, and the liquid splashed to the ground, releasing a pungent, acrid scent that clawed at my senses. A wave of dizziness hit me, and I staggered back, the room spinning.

Evelyn's laughter cut through the chaos, sharp and triumphant. "You'll succumb, just like all the others. Dionysus feeds on your pain, your weakness. You were always meant for this."

As we grappled, our bodies collided violently, the space around us distorting. Walls warped, shifting from sterile laboratories to dark, claustrophobic chambers. Every step we took dragged us deeper into a nightmarish labyrinth of twisted memories.

The locket pulsed against my chest, its warmth fighting the cold grip of her influence, urging me to resist. But then, with a jarring crash, we tumbled into another room—the altar room.

The rancid stench of death hit me, and my stomach turned. My heart plummeted as I caught sight of the skeletal remains bound to the altar—Ms. Pachi, still locked in her final, agonized moments. Her empty eye sockets seemed to bore into me, a silent accusation.

"This is where it all began," Evelyn whispered. She rose from the floor slowly, relishing in the torment she had created. "You can't outrun this, Harold. Dionysus demands sacrifice, and you... you've been running from it your entire life."

I couldn't breathe. The memory of Ms. Pachi's screams echoes in my ears.

Evelyn's gaze turned cruel, a twisted smile tugging at her lips. "You think you're free, don't you? That you can fight me, fight *him*? Look at her, Harold. Look at what you did."

"That wasn't me!" My voice cracked. "I was a kid—I was manipulated! I didn't know what I was doing!"

Her laughter was cold, devoid of any warmth. "Still clinging to that pathetic excuse? You think denying the truth will absolve you? You chose this, just like you chose Emily."

Emily's name sent a fresh wave of anger through me. My mind raced with memories—her gentle smile, the way she'd comfort me, her promise to escape together. How could she be part of this madness?

"You're lying," I spat, but the weight of Evelyn's words tightened like a vice around my chest. The altar loomed behind her, a reminder of the horrors I couldn't outrun.

Evelyn stepped closer; her eyes gleaming with triumph. "You've always been too blind to see the truth. But now... Now it's all unraveling."

The locket burned hot against my skin, the only thing keeping me grounded as the memories crashed over me. I clenched my fists until my nails bit into my palms, desperate to hold onto anything that wasn't her voice or the horrors around me.

"You belong to Dionysus," she whispered, venom dripping from every word. "You always have."

The Ultimate Betrayal

"EMILY."

The woman I thought I loved. The one I believed needed saving. How could she have been a part of this?

My eyes flicked back to Ms. Pachi, lying on the altar; her skeletal remains were a haunting reminder of the darkness that had consumed me. Ms. Pachi had been kind to me—so kind. When I was a child, lost in a world I didn't understand, she had always been there, her gentle smile welcoming me with warmth and safety. She'd encourage me when I was down, guiding me like a second mother. Her soft eyes were filled with care, and now, staring at her twisted remains, that memory cut deep, like a blade sinking into my chest.

And I had killed her.

Manipulated into taking her life by the forces I was now trying to fight. Guilt slammed into me, suffocating, as the weight of my actions grew unbearable. I'd taken away the life of someone who had only ever been good to me. How could I have let it come to this? I should have protected her—cherished her, not become the instrument of her death. Not the puppet of those who wielded power over me.

Tears stung my eyes, and I dropped to my knees, my breath ragged. "I'm so sorry," I whispered to her remains, my voice trembling. "I'm so, so sorry." The realization that I had ended her life, that her kindness had been repaid with cruelty, tore at me. She was gone—forever gone—because of me.

And Emily…

I thought I had fought for her, for someone innocent, for someone I believed was like Ms. Pachi—kind, pure, and deserving of protection. I had convinced myself that she was the light in the dark. But now, all of it felt like a twisted illusion—a mirage carefully crafted to lead me down this dark path.

I trusted her. And in that trust, I had allowed the people behind this to pull me deeper into their nightmare. I had opened my heart to her, but she was the one orchestrating this chaos. She betrayed me.

Evelyn's voice slithered through my thoughts, sharp and taunting. "It's tragic, isn't it?" she purred. "Ms. Pachi, so sweet, so loyal. And what did she get in return? Your blade against her skin. Emily's here, Harold. Still pulling your strings, still playing her part. Ms. Pachi… Well, her death was just a necessary sacrifice, wasn't it? You did what you were *meant* to do."

My chest tightened, the guilt turning to nausea. I clutched the locket, its warmth barely cutting through the ice in my veins. Ms. Pachi had died because of them. Because of me.

I closed my eyes, the tears finally spilling down my cheeks. "I didn't know," I rasped, my voice rough. "I didn't know." Yet, even as I said it, the words rang empty. How many lives had I shattered in my blind faith, in my ignorance?

Ms. Pachi. Emily. Me.

They had all been destroyed—each in their own way—by this place. And now Emily was the one still standing—not the woman I had once loved, but something far darker. Something twisted beyond recognition.

And Ms. Pachi was gone, lost forever to this nightmare.

I clenched my fists, trying to hold onto the last vestiges of control, but Evelyn's laughter echoed around me, a mocking, cruel sound. "Face it, Harold," she sneered. "You're nothing more than a pawn. Always have been. You killed her, and you'll kill again."

I couldn't breathe. The weight of it all was crushing me. Ms. Pachi's empty eye sockets seemed to stare back at me, a silent accusation. And I had no defense. No excuses.

Only guilt.

With every ounce of strength I had left, I fought to push away the tide of despair. I could either succumb to this darkness or rise against it. But first, I needed to escape—away from Evelyn's twisted triumph and away from the memories that threatened to drown me.

I closed my eyes, letting the warmth of the locket pulse against my chest, urging me to focus and find clarity amid the chaos. I had to remember who I was beneath the weight of all this loss.

"Emily was never yours to save," Evelyn continued, her smile cold and triumphant. "You were nothing but her pawn."

I didn't lash out. I didn't scream or deny it. The truth was already starting to crystallize in my mind, and no amount of yelling would change what I was now seeing more clearly. The signs had been there all along—the inconsistencies, the subtle ways Emily had drawn me into this madness.

"Go on," I said, my voice strained but steady. Part of me wanted to reject everything Evelyn was saying, but I had come too far to ignore the truth any longer. The pieces were falling into place.

Evelyn's laughter was sharp. "Finally, you're listening. Good. You were always so stubborn, Harold." Her eyes gleamed with satisfaction. "Emily orchestrated everything—the kidnapping, the sanatorium, even the journal. She wanted you to find it, to follow her trail like a dog chasing a bone. And you did, exactly as she planned."

"The journal," I murmured, more to myself than to Evelyn. "She always kept it close..."

"Exactly." Evelyn's voice slithered through the air, wrapping around my thoughts. "That wasn't an accident. She knew you would see it; follow its breadcrumbs to this very moment. It was never about saving her—it was about you reuniting with the locket's power."

The locket. The object that had tied me to this place, to this twisted history of darkness.

"Emily needed you," Evelyn went on, her tone softening into something almost mockingly sympathetic. "But not in the way you thought. She didn't need saving, Harold. She needed you to embrace your connection to the locket and bring its power back into play. And you did exactly that."

I felt my stomach tighten, but I didn't recoil. A small part of me still struggled to reconcile this version of Emily—the manipulative mastermind—with the woman I had loved, but the rest of me was understanding. She had used me to fulfill a vision that reached beyond my comprehension.

"Why?" I asked, my voice low, almost hollow. "Why go through all this? What does she want with the locket's power?"

Evelyn's smile widened, revealing the depths of her twisted satisfaction. "You still don't grasp it, do you? She wants control over more than just her own fate. Emily seeks to awaken the ancient forces tied to that locket—forces of chaos and ecstasy. It's a key, Harold, a key to unleashing Dionysian power. And Emily? She's one of the few who truly understands what that means. You were merely the final piece she needed to complete her ritual."

I stood there, silent, allowing her words to wash over me. The world didn't feel like it was spinning anymore, but it wasn't steady either. Emily had manipulated me—yes—but for a purpose far grander than simple betrayal. I was seeing the terrifying scope of her ambition and the darkness it unleashed sent shivers down my spine.

"So, what happens now?" I asked, meeting Evelyn's gaze. "What's the next step?"

Evelyn's smile was a mixture of amusement and admiration. "Ah, Harold. That's what I like about you—you don't flinch when faced with the truth. The next step? Well, that depends on you. Do you want to embrace the role you've been playing all along? Or do you want to walk away now, knowing you were nothing more than a pawn in Emily's game?"

I didn't answer right away. I wasn't sure I even knew the answer yet. But one thing was clear: I wasn't walking away. Not now. Not after everything. I needed to see this through to understand what Emily's endgame was. If I'd been a pawn, then maybe it was time to see what happened when the pawn stopped following the rules.

"I'm not going anywhere," I said quietly, my voice firm. "But I'm done being a pawn."

Evelyn's eyes flickered with approval, though her smile remained cruel. "Oh, Harold, you're finally catching on. But don't worry—you'll learn the rest soon enough. Emily will be so pleased to see how far you've come."

The mention of Emily sent a pang of something—regret? Betrayal? —through me, but I shoved it down. I had made my choice. Whatever the truth was, whatever Emily's true motives, I would find out soon enough. And when I did, I would decide what to do with it.

But now, staring into Evelyn's eyes, my mind swirled with questions, doubts... and something deeper. I wasn't ready to face it all yet. Not here. Not with her watching, feeding off my confusion like a predator. I needed space—somewhere to think. Somewhere beyond Evelyn's grasp.

My fingers instinctively brushed against the locket, its cold metal pressing into my palm. I didn't even realize I was clutching it, seeking some clarity from its presence. And then it hit me—an escape, a way to leave this confrontation, if only for a moment.

Evelyn's voice cut through my thoughts. "What's the matter, Harold? Don't tell me you're having second thoughts." She smirked, sensing my hesitation. "I thought you were done playing the fool."

I met her gaze, but inside, a different decision was forming. I would not let her dictate how this ended. Not now. Not after everything.

"I need to think," I said abruptly, stepping back, my hand gripping the locket tighter. Evelyn's smirk faltered, her eyes narrowing.

"Think? What's there to think about?" Her voice sharpened with irritation, her control slipping. "You finally understand the truth, Harold. This is what you wanted—answers. Now you're running away?"

Her mocking tone was a thin veil for the frustration bubbling beneath the surface. I could see it and feel it in the way her smile faltered. She had expected me to fall in line and accept my role, but I wasn't ready to do that. Not yet.

"I'm not running away," I replied, keeping my voice even. "I just need time to figure this out."

Evelyn's eyes blazed with anger, the triumph that had been in her gaze moments ago now turning cold and hard. "You don't get to think, Harold. Not anymore. You're in this now. You either accept your place or you fall."

The air crackled with tension, but I stood my ground. My heart pounded in my chest as I stepped back, my thumb pressing harder into the locket's surface. I wasn't going to fall. Not yet.

"Goodbye, Evelyn," I whispered, and with that, I twisted the locket in my hand, feeling a pulse of energy surge through me.

The room around me began to warp, twisting and blurring as the edges of reality seemed to fold in on themselves. Evelyn's face contorted in fury as she lunged forward, her fingers outstretched to grab me.

"You can't run from this, Harold!" she screamed, her voice distorting as the locket's power dragged me away. "You'll come back! You have to come back!"

But her words faded into the world around me, and suddenly, I was back in the greenhouse.

CHAPTER 19

The Locket's Curse

The night weighed heavily on my chest as I sat alone in the greenhouse, clutching the locket in my hand. My mind swirled with everything that had happened—Emily, the locket, the unspoken guilt that gnawed at me like a festering wound. I squeezed the locket tighter, feeling its cool metal against my palm. The locket had become a symbol of everything I couldn't escape—a source of chaos that had pulled me into darkness, even as it had helped me navigate the most perilous moments.

My eyelids drooped, the exhaustion pulling me under, but just as sleep began to claim me, I felt something shift—a sudden, dizzying drop, like the floor beneath me had collapsed. When I opened my eyes, the world was no longer mine.

I was standing in a vast, empty field, the sky above me sickly yellow, the color of old bruises. The air crackled with electricity, and the ground beneath my feet scorched and blackened. Everything felt... off. The horizon stretched too far, the sky hung too low, and the shadows... moved.

In the distance, I could see a small, fragile figure approaching me— Emily. But she wasn't walking; she was gliding, her feet never touching the ground. Her eyes were locked on me, unblinking and empty. I tried to call out to her, but my voice was swallowed by the air, muffled, as if I were underwater.

Suddenly, the sky began to twist and warp, the clouds churning violently above. I looked down at my hands and the locket—it wasn't there. Instead, my fingers were smeared with blood, thick and warm, dripping between my knuckles. Panic surged through my body. I wiped my hands on my shirt, but the blood wouldn't come off. It spread, staining everything and seeping into my skin.

"Harold."

Her voice cut through the silence. I looked up, and Emily was closer now, her face pale and hollow, like a porcelain doll with cracks spider-webbing across her cheeks. Her eyes—God, those eyes—they weren't hers anymore. They were dark, empty voids, pulling everything in. I felt myself falling into them, drowning in the weight of her gaze.

"You left me," she whispered, and this time, the words sliced through me.

"I didn't," I choked out. "I tried to—"

"You failed."

The words echoed in the sky, repeated by the clouds, the wind, and the ground. My heart pounded, each beat growing louder, more frantic. The field around us began to shift and change. The scorched earth gave way to a graveyard, rows upon rows of tombstones stretching endlessly in every direction. Names were etched into the stones; some were familiar and haunting—my birth mother, Samantha, Emily, my biological father, Adam Morgan, and Ms. Pachi.

The shadows moved again, slithering between the graves, coiling around my legs, tightening like chains. I struggled, trying to break free, but they were relentless, pulling me down, inch by inch. The sky above grew darker, thick clouds swirling into a vortex, black as ink, blocking out what little light remained.

Out of the corner of my eye, I saw Emily again—closer now, standing right beside me. Her face, inches from mine, was pale and hollow, her breath cold as it brushed my skin. The smile that once brought comfort was twisted now—mocking, cruel.

"You think you can run from this, Harold?" Her voice wasn't hers anymore, either. It had an edge, sharp and taunting. *"You're a coward. You always were."*

My chest tightened, my breath coming in short, ragged bursts. "I'm not," I stammered, but the words felt wrong, forced, hollow. "I didn't mean—"

"You didn't mean to kill me?" She lashed out, venomous, her eyes darkening into voids of accusation. Her features twisted, shifting into something grotesque—something monstrous. *"You didn't mean to let us all die?"*

I froze. She wasn't dead. She couldn't be dead. My mind raced, clinging to the reality I knew—Emily was alive, wasn't she? But the shadows, the locket—everything was wrong. Wasn't it?

The shadows tightened their grip, dragging me down into the Earth, cold, damp soil pressing against my skin. I could smell the decay of the graveyard as it enveloped me, pulling me deeper. Panic came over me as I reached for Emily—for anyone—but my hands met only emptiness. The locket, the cursed thing, now embedded into my chest, pulsed with a sickening rhythm, each throb echoing the pounding of my heart.

But Emily—why did I still reach for her? Why did I give in so easily? I didn't trust her anymore. I knew that. Yet, something in me still sought her approval; I still longed to believe in the version of her I once knew. And I hated myself for it.

Suddenly, the ground beneath me gave way entirely, and I was falling—falling through endless darkness and through memories I had buried deep. My failures, my regrets, everything I wanted to forget came rushing at me, each more painful than the last. Emily's voice followed me, echoing through the void, growing louder and more accusing with each passing moment.

"You could have saved me."

"I tried," I whispered, my voice breaking.

"You didn't try hard enough." Her words struck like a dagger, twisting deeper.

And then, searing pain shot through me—the locket, burning against my skin, branding me from the inside. I screamed, the white-hot agony tearing through my chest, my throat raw from the effort. I could feel it now, pulsing and tightening around my heart; its cold metal constricting, squeezing the life out of me.

The darkness shifted again, and I found myself back in the greenhouse. But this wasn't the place I remembered. The plants that once bloomed here were withered and dead; their leaves blackened and curled in on themselves. The air was thick with the stench of rot, suffocating and cloying. And the locket—oh, God, the locket— wasn't in my hand anymore. I could feel it inside me, like a parasite burrowing into my soul, its tendrils wrapping tighter and tighter around my heart.

I collapsed to the ground, gasping for air, my chest heaving with the effort. I needed to breathe. I needed to get this thing out of me. But the locket's presence was inescapable, its power more insidious than ever. I could hear it now, clearer than before—a voice, low and persuasive, whispering from the dark corners of my mind.

"Use me."

"No," I muttered, shaking my head, desperate to block it out. But the voice—its voice—was persistent.

"You need me."

The world flickered around me, the dead plants rustling as if moved by an invisible hand, the wind carrying their dry, crumbling leaves.

But why did I still feel a pull toward Emily? Why did her presence still grip me, even now, after everything? I didn't trust her anymore —I hadn't for a long time. Yet, at that moment, I didn't know why I couldn't let her go. Why did I let the thought of her consume me? Was it the locket manipulating my thoughts, bending my will to its own? Or was it my weakness, my desperation to hold on to something familiar, even if it was twisted beyond recognition?

"You'll never be free of this," she whispered, her voice cutting through the haze, cold and absolute.

Then, just as suddenly as she had appeared, she vanished, dissolving into the shadows and leaving me alone.

Alone, but not free. Never free.

The locket's weight pressed down on me. Without it, I would be vulnerable—exposed. Yet, with it, I was losing myself. I could feel its power seeping into me, making me see things, bending my mind, and controlling my thoughts. But how could I give it up? It was all I had now. It was the only thing standing between me and the chaos of the world. The only thing that made me feel like I still had control, even as it drove me to the edge of insanity.

I could feel the cold metal tightening its grip around my heart, and for the first time, I wasn't sure if I had the strength to fight it. I wasn't sure if I even wanted to.

The world around me flickered, the greenhouse melting away as if it had never been there, and I woke up gasping, my body drenched in sweat. My fingers were still wrapped around the locket; its weight was heavy in my palm, but I held onto it tighter than before.

I couldn't give it up. Not now.

I gasped for air, chest heaving, but the crushing weight of the dream clung like a second skin. Emily's voice echoed in my skull, sharper now, piercing through whatever remnants of sleep were left. The graveyard, the blood—they felt real. Too real. But as I blinked, the twisted world of shadows faded, leaving me alone in the greenhouse.

Sweat dripped from my forehead as I staggered to my feet, every muscle aching like I'd been running for miles. The locket's presence throbbed against my chest, and I swear I could feel it pulsing—alive like it was part of me now. I pressed my hand to where the cool metal had dug itself in, an unsettling comfort blooming from its touch.

"What the hell was that?" I muttered, rubbing my face with shaky hands.

Was it a nightmare? Or something more? It didn't feel like a warning. No, it felt like something was *testing* me, seeing how far I could go before I broke.

My reflection caught in the broken glass of the greenhouse windows. Hollow eyes, skin pale as death, and black hair slicked to my forehead. I barely recognized the man staring back at me. A stranger. Or maybe... this is who I'd been all along, and I hadn't seen it yet.

But I wasn't scared anymore. Not of the locket. Not of the voices. Not of the madness. What scared me was the idea of letting it go.

The locket hummed again; its rhythm synced with my heartbeat. And despite everything it had shown me, despite the twisted visions and the gut-wrenching guilt that gnawed at me, I couldn't help but feel... *stronger*.

I closed my eyes, trying to shake the last of the dream away, but Emily's voice still lingered. **You failed.**

No. I didn't fail. Not yet. And I wasn't going to.

The locket gave me power—real power. Sure, it was driving me insane, tearing at the seams of my mind with every passing minute.

I rubbed my eyes and stared at the faint light spilling through the shattered panes above. The dream wasn't a warning. It was showing me what I already knew deep down. I needed the locket.

The madness? That was the price. But if I could harness it, control it... I might make things right. Maybe I could *fix* everything.

I took a deep breath, feeling the weight in my chest grow heavier, the locket pressing against my heart like it was sinking deeper into me. But I wasn't afraid. Not anymore. I wasn't fighting it. Not like before.

"I can control it," I whispered. My voice sounded hollow, echoing off the glass walls.

The locket seemed to respond with a slow, steady pulse that matched the certainty growing in me. This was my key. I could finally have the power to change things—to take back control.

I clenched my fists, staring at the wreckage around me. The dead plants, the shattered glass—it didn't matter anymore. None of it mattered. The chaos? The voices? They were part of the deal. And I was ready to accept that now.

The locket thrummed again, soothing almost as if it were rewarding me for my decision. The madness would come. It always did. But I would not run from it anymore. I would not let it break me.

I'd use it. I'd bend it to my will. I'd *own* it.

With a final glance at the ghost in the glass—at the broken man I used to be—I turned away from the light. The outside world was still waiting for me. But this time, I wouldn't face it empty-handed.

The locket was mine now. And whatever darkness it brought, I'd carry it. I'd survive it.

CHAPTER 20

Emily's Endgame

I stood in the greenhouse, my breath steadying as the locket pulsed against my chest, the rhythm now in perfect harmony with my heartbeat. I'd made my choice. I wasn't fighting the locket anymore; I was embracing it. Its power coursed through me, buzzing in my veins, making the world around me seem fragile and distant.

I closed my eyes, and when I opened them, the greenhouse had shifted. Not gradually, but in an instant—as if reality itself had blinked. In front of me was a door, wooden and worn, with chipped paint and rusted hinges. It stood where there had been nothing before, its presence commanding and unnatural. The locket hummed with approval, urging me forward.

Without hesitation, I stepped through.

The air on the other side was thick with decay. I recognized the smell immediately—stale, rotting wood mixed with damp stone, the distinct scent of the sanatorium. I was back, but this wasn't the past. No. This was real, the present, the sanatorium in its ruined state. The walls were crumbling, water stains streaked the ceiling, and the windows were boarded up, blocking out what little daylight remained. It felt as though the place itself had been forgotten, abandoned to rot, like the people who had once been trapped inside.

I ran my fingers along the cracked plaster, the rough texture grounding me in the moment. This wasn't a dream, and it wasn't the locket twisting my perception. It was real. The door had brought me back here. But why? I had no idea. The locket thrummed, guiding me, but I didn't know where it was leading me or who—or what—I would find.

I started walking, my footsteps echoing against the decaying floors, the sound bouncing off the empty walls like a heartbeat. The deeper I went, the heavier the air felt. I couldn't shake the feeling that I wasn't alone, but I wasn't sure if it was my paranoia or the locket making me more attuned to the weight of the place.

Another door appeared just ahead of me out of nowhere. I should've been unnerved, but I wasn't. The locket had a purpose, and I was part of it now. It was showing me the way. Without hesitation, I reached for the handle and pushed it open.

Inside, the room was even worse than the hallway—peeling paint, exposed wires, and broken furniture scattered across the floor. The air was stagnant, filled with dust and the faint smell of mildew. But in the center of it all, standing still, was Emily.

She turned to face me slowly, her eyes locking onto mine with a strange calmness that sent a chill down my spine. This wasn't a reunion. It was something darker.

"Harold," she said softly, stepping forward with that same knowing smile, the one that had always drawn me in and made me feel seen and loved. "You came back to me."

My throat tightened. "Emily..." I whispered, unsure of how to proceed. I wasn't even sure why I was here. The locket had brought me, but for what purpose? "What is this?"

She smiled—a chilling, sweet smile that didn't reach her eyes. "This, my love, is the culmination of everything. Everything I've been waiting for."

I stepped back, confused, the locket thumping against my chest. "I don't understand."

"You will," she said, her voice honeyed yet cold. She moved closer, her fingers grazing my arm. Her touch was soft and familiar, yet it sent a chill down my spine. "I've always known what this place could be. What *we* could be. I grew up here, Harold. My mother taught me the ways of Dionysus and prepared me to carry on her legacy."

Her voice was steady, but there was a dangerous glint in her eyes now. "The sanatorium was never just about healing. It was about unlocking the true potential of human fear and ecstasy. My mother understood that, and so do I. The rituals, the experiments—they weren't cruel; they were *freeing*. Dionysus showed us the way."

My stomach twisted. "Emily… What are you saying?"

She stepped toward me, her hand resting against my chest, over the locket. Her eyes softened, almost as if she were trying to comfort me, trying to make me believe she still cared. "I'm saying, Harold, that we have a chance—*you* have a chance—to finish what they started. To recreate the world. A world where we can let go and give ourselves fully to the pleasure and to the freedom that Dionysus promised."

Her words made my head spin. "You... you want to use the locket to control people?"

"No, Harold," she whispered, her lips brushing against my ear now, her voice thick with seduction. "Not control. *Free*. Imagine a world where people can live in eternal ecstasy. That's what the locket can do. It's the key to unlocking the sanatorium's power—its *true* power."

I pulled back, my heart pounding in my chest. "You're talking about chaos. That's not freedom, Emily. That's madness."

Her smile faded, her eyes hardening. "Don't you see, Harold? We've been trapped in a world of suffering for too long. This is our chance to break free from all of that. To create something new—something beautiful."

I shook my head, stepping back as the weight of her words sank in. "You… you were using me this whole time."

She didn't deny it. Instead, she stepped closer again, brushing her hand against my cheek. "I needed you to unlock the locket's power, yes. But we can still do this together, Harold. You and me, just like before."

Her touch was soft, and for a moment, I felt myself slipping. I wanted to believe her, wanted to give in to the warmth of her body, to the comfort she was offering. I had always needed her—*wanted* her. And now, at this moment, with the locket's power thrumming between us, I could feel that pull more than ever.

"Harold," she whispered, her lips inches from mine. "We can have everything. The world is at our feet. You don't have to be afraid anymore. I'll take care of you, just like I always have."

My mind was spinning, torn between desire and the cold truth I had seen. "No, no, this isn't right."

Her eyes darkened, the sweetness in her voice turning sharp. "You need me, Harold. You always have. Without me, you're nothing. You can't escape this."

I swallowed hard, feeling the locket pulsing harder. She moved in closer, her hand sliding down to my waist, fingertips teasingly trailing along the fabric of my pants before unzipping them. "Just give in," she purred, her breath hot against my skin. "Let me take the pain away."

And for a moment, I almost did. Her lips brushed against mine, and my body responded, aching for the warmth and comfort she promised. But then I felt it—the darkness behind her words. The coldness beneath her touch. This wasn't love. It wasn't even lust. It was control.

"No," I said, my voice barely more than a whisper, but it was enough. I stepped back, breaking the connection. "You don't love me. You're using me. You always were."

Her eyes flashed with anger, her seductive façade cracking. "You're weak, Harold," she hissed. "You always have been."

I clenched my fists, feeling the locket's power surge through me, stronger now than before. "Maybe," I said, my voice steady now. "But I'm not weak enough to let you destroy everything."

Her face twisted with rage, and the sanatorium seemed to shift around us, the walls warping and twisting as her anger grew. "You think you can stop me?" she snarled. "You think you can control this power without me?"

I focused on the locket, feeling its energy pulsing through me. "I don't need to control it," I said. "I just need to use it against you."

With a final surge of will, I pushed back against her, the locket's power flooding the room. Emily screamed as the sanatorium began to warp and twist, the walls shifting and bending around her. I could see the fear in her eyes now—desperation.

"You can't fight me, Harold. You never could. You've always been weak. Always running to me for comfort, for love. You think you can stand against me now?" Her words hit like daggers, piercing into my deepest fears. "You're nothing without me."

The room continued to warp and twist, reflections of my darkest memories flashing before my eyes—moments of doubt, of failure, and of loneliness. Images of Emily comforting me, holding me, and promising me the world. My knees buckled, my heart racing as the weight of it all crushed me.

I could feel her feeding on my weakness, pushing me to the edge.

"You're mine, Harold," she whispered, stepping closer. "You've always been mine."

"No…" I muttered, but my voice was weak. The images around me were overwhelming, the pain suffocating. Emily's presence was everywhere—her voice in my head, her hands on my skin. She was right—I was weak. I had always needed her.

But then, through the chaos, I felt it—the locket. Its power thrummed against my chest, a steady pulse grounding me. It was stronger than her. I was stronger than her.

"You're wrong," I said, my voice shaking but steady. I focused on the locket, drawing its power into me, feeling it surge through my veins. "You're not real. *This* isn't real."

Her eyes widened as I pressed my hand to the locket, using its power to push back against the illusions she had created. The images around me began to flicker, the twisted walls of the sanatorium shaking, trembling under the weight of the locket's energy.

Emily screamed as I pushed harder, the locket's power overwhelming her illusions. I could see it now—the cracks in her mask, the fear in her eyes. "You can't do this!" she shrieked, backing away as the room began to shift again, this time under my control.

"I can," I said, my voice growing stronger. "I know what you're afraid of, Emily."

Her eyes blazed with fury, but I saw the fear lurking beneath. She had always been afraid. Afraid of being alone. Afraid of losing control. Afraid of her mother.

I twisted the locket's power, forcing her own fears and memories back at her. Visions of her past flooded the room—her mother's cruel experiments, the rituals she had been forced to endure, the pain she had hidden behind her cold, calculated smile.

"No!" she screamed, collapsing as the weight of her memories crashed down on her.

I didn't wait. With a final surge of power, I dispelled the last of her illusions, and the door appeared behind me. I turned away from her, leaving her to face the darkness of her own making, and stepped through the door.

CHAPTER 21

The Price of Truth

The door slammed shut behind me, and I stood in the cold, empty hallway once again. The twisted reality Emily had woven around me was gone, but the oppressive air of the sanatorium lingered like a heavy fog. Every fiber of my being told me to run, to get as far away from this place as possible. But something held me back.

The locket, still pulsing with an energy I could barely comprehend, felt heavier than ever against my chest. My fingers brushed its surface, and a low hum vibrated through me. Ahead of me—deeper into the heart of the sanatorium—lay the truth. The truth I had come so close to uncovering but had never fully grasped.

I knew I had a choice.

I could leave now. I could walk out of here with my life, with my mind still mostly intact. But I would never know what really happened in this place. I would never understand the full scope of what had been done, to me and to so many others. The weight of that ignorance pressed down on me, heavier than any physical burden.

I turned and faced the shadows that stretched out before me. Some-where down those halls lay the answers—the truth.

But was I willing to pay the price for it?

My hand clenched around the locket, and its hum grew louder, almost insistent. It was as if the sanatorium itself was calling, pulling me deeper into its depths. My heart raced, torn between the primal urge to flee and the equally powerful need to understand. Emily had fallen, her illusions shattered—but her power still lingered. The locket had shown me glimpses of the past, but there was more. There had to be more.

I stepped forward. Then another. The air seemed to thicken around me as though the sanatorium itself was closing in, swallowing me whole. But I forced myself to move deeper into the bowels of the building, past the ruined rooms and decayed hallways that now felt more like a living organism than a structure.

As I moved further in, the walls shifted, almost imperceptibly at first. The shadows seemed to twist, warping into strange, misshapen forms. My skin prickled, my instincts screaming I was crossing a point of no return. But still, I walked forward, driven by something deeper than fear.

And then I saw it.

At the end of the hallway, where the walls met in jagged angles, there was a door I had never noticed before. It was small, almost hidden, as though it didn't belong to the rest of the building. I should have ignored it. I should have turned around and left.

But the locket thrummed harder against my chest, and suddenly, I remembered.

I had been here before—as a child. The memory was faint, buried under years of repression, but it was there. This door wasn't new—it was old. *Ancient,* even. I had walked this path once before, years ago, when the sanatorium had still been alive with its experiments. I had been here, and I had gone through that door.

A chill ran down my spine, and I hesitated. The truth lay beyond that door—I could feel it. But at what cost? What would I find on the other side? I looked back toward the way I had come, toward the exit that could lead me back to safety. I could still leave. I could still walk away.

But I couldn't. I had to know.

With a deep breath, I turned the handle and pushed the door open. The hinges groaned, and a waft of cold air rushed out, thick with the stench of mildew and decay. Beyond the door lay a stairwell, spiraling downward into darkness. My legs felt heavy as I descended, each step bringing me closer to something I wasn't sure I was ready to face.

The walls around me dripped with moisture, and the air grew colder the further down I went. It was as if the sanatorium itself was sinking into the Earth, descending into some forgotten, buried past. At the bottom of the stairs, I found another hallway, this one much narrower and lined with doors on either side.

A memory flashed before my eyes—doors like these, patients locked behind them, screaming in agony as the experiments took place. And there I was, a child, watching it all, feeling... nothing.

The locket pulsed, and the memory twisted. I was no longer just watching—I was *participating*. My hands, small and trembling, pressed the locket against one of the patient's heads, watching as their screams filled the air. I had used the locket's power on them, bending their minds, warping their thoughts. I had been a part of it all.

I staggered back, the horror of the memory crashing over me. "No... no, that can't be right," I muttered, clutching the locket tightly. But deep down, I knew it was true. I had willingly taken part in the experiments. I hadn't been a victim—I had been complicit.

My heart pounded as I stumbled through the hallway, my mind reeling. I had been a child, yes, but I had made a choice. I had used the locket's power, knowing full well the pain it would cause. The sanatorium had warped me and twisted me, just as it had twisted everyone else within its walls.

Suddenly, a figure appeared in front of me—a small boy, no more than six or seven. His face was pale, his eyes wide and empty. He looked at me with a hollow stare, and I realized with a jolt who he was.

He was *me*.

My younger self beckoned, the cruel smile widening as he turned and walked down the hallway. His small footsteps echoed ominously in the suffocating silence, his pale figure a ghost of the boy I had once been. I wanted to run—run far away from that twisted reflection of my past. But I couldn't. The locket throbbed against my chest, its power pulling me forward, deeper into the blackened core of the sanatorium.

The final room loomed at the end of the corridor, its door slightly ajar, as though it had been waiting for me all this time. My younger self slipped through the door without hesitation, disappearing into the shadows inside.

I hesitated, my hand trembling as I reached for the handle. Something terrible was waiting beyond that threshold—something I wasn't sure I could face. But I had to. I had to know the truth... even if it destroyed me.

I pushed the door open and stepped inside.

The room was cold—so cold it felt like the air was biting into my skin. The walls were lined with old, rusted medical equipment, tables, and cabinets scattered haphazardly, covered in dust and decay. And in the center of the room, illuminated by a sickly, flickering light, stood my younger self, waiting for me.

"Do you remember this place?" he asked, his voice unnaturally calm. His eyes, those hollow, empty eyes, bore into me.

I shook my head. "No... I—" The words caught in my throat as something stirred in the back of my mind—a memory, faint and distant, clawing its way to the surface. I had been here before. The room, the smell of disinfectant mixed with something far worse— blood, rot, fear—was all familiar.

"You don't want to remember, but you do," my younger self said, stepping toward me. His small hand reached up, brushing the locket around my neck. "Let me show you."

Before I could react, the room shifted, the walls bending and warping until they were no longer the dilapidated remnants of a forgotten past. The space around me transformed, pulling me back into a time when the sanatorium was alive, its halls echoing with the cries of the broken and the damned.

I stood in the room again, but it was different. The air was sharp with the scent of antiseptic and something more metallic. Medical tables gleamed under the bright fluorescent lights, sterile and cold. A woman stood in the center of the room, her back to me. Evelyn.

Her voice was calm and clinical as she spoke to someone hidden from view. "You understand what needs to be done. We can't have any more mistakes, Emily. The brain is fragile, but if we can rewire his thoughts and make him forget what he's done, we can harness the power of the locket for our purposes."

Emily.

She stepped forward, a shadow emerging from the corner. Her face was younger and softer, and her eyes were wide with uncertainty and fear. "But Harold—he's just a boy, Mama. He doesn't understand—"

Evelyn whirled on her, her patience snapping. In a swift motion, she grabbed Emily around the neck, her grip firm but not crushing. "Don't ever call me 'Mama' again," she hissed, holding her gaze with a fierce intensity. After a heartbeat, she let Emily go and began straightening her lab coat.

"That's exactly why he's perfect," she continued, her voice low but filled with conviction. "He doesn't understand, but he can be made to obey. You will do what you're told, Emily, or do I need to remind you what's at stake here?"

Emily's face paled, and she looked down, nodding silently. She didn't dare argue. My younger self was standing in the corner, watching with the same empty stare he had shown me earlier. I could feel the locket pulsing against my chest, syncing with the rhythm of the memory.

My breath caught in my throat as the scene shifted again. This time, I was standing in front of a glass wall, looking into another room—an operating room. On the table lay a patient, strapped down, struggling weakly against the restraints. His face was contorted in pain, eyes wide with terror as wires and electrodes were connected to his skull.

I was there, too. My younger self, standing beside Evelyn. The locket glowed in his small hand, the energy from its flowing through the electrodes into the patient's brain. I could see the man's body convulse as the power surged into him, his thoughts—his very mind—being torn apart by the locket's influence. His memories were being rewritten, rearranged, and then erased, leaving nothing but a blank, hollow shell.

"Do it, Harold," Evelyn commanded, her voice sharp and unyielding. "You have to *push*. Use the locket. Break him."

My younger self hesitated, his small hands trembling as he clutched the locket. "But… it hurts him."

Evelyn's hand landed on his shoulder, her grip firm, nails digging into his skin. "You're not hurting him, Harold. You're *fixing* him. He's sick, and this is the only way to help him."

My heart pounded in my chest as I watched the scene unfold, my stomach twisting with nausea. I had known, even as a child, that something was wrong. But I had trusted her. I had believed her when she said we were helping them. I believed *Emily* when she told me this was all for the greater good.

Emily stepped forward, placing her hand over my younger self's. "It's okay, Harold," she whispered, her voice soft but edged with fear. "Just... just do what she says. You are helping him."

The locket flared with power in my younger self's hand, and the man on the table screamed, his voice raw, agonized. The sound was like nails on glass, and I felt bile rise in my throat.

This wasn't right. This had never been right.

But I had done it.

I had done exactly what Evelyn had wanted.

The memory shattered, and I was back in the room with my younger self. He was staring at me, his eyes no longer hollow but filled with something far worse—recognition. He knew what we had done... what *I* had done.

"You enjoyed it," he said, his voice cold and cruel. "You liked using the locket, didn't you? Watching them break."

I staggered back, shaking my head. "No. I didn't. I didn't know—"

But I had known. Deep down, I knew.

Another memory crashed over me, pulling me under its dark tide.

I was standing in a ritual chamber, deep within the sanatorium, surrounded by symbols drawn in blood. Evelyn stood at the altar, holding the locket high, its light casting eerie shadows across the walls. Emily was there too, her face pale, hands trembling as she held a book open before her, chanting in a language I didn't understand.

On the floor before the altar lay a patient, bound in chains, his eyes wide with terror as he writhed against the restraints. The locket pulsed with dark energy, its power feeding off the ritual and the fear and pain of the man below.

Evelyn's voice rang out, sharp and commanding. "The locket needs more, Harold. You have to give it more. Only then will we unlock its true potential."

I stepped forward, the locket in my hand, drawn to the power it offered. I was a child, but the power it promised was intoxicating and overwhelming. I could feel the man's fear, his desperation, feeding into me through the locket, and I raised it high, ready to give Evelyn what she wanted.

But just before I could, the man looked at me—right at me—and whispered, "Please."

Something inside me snapped.

I couldn't do it. I dropped the locket and ran, ran as fast as I could, away from the altar, away from Evelyn, away from the horrors she had made me a part of. But it was too late. The locket had taken hold of me. It had already twisted me, just as it had twisted them.

The memory faded, and I was back in the room again, the weight of what I had done crashing down on me. My younger self watched me, his expression unreadable.

"I didn't mean to," I whispered, tears burning in my eyes.

But my younger self just smiled—that same cruel smile that had haunted me all my life.

"Yes, you did."

CHAPTER 22

The Escape Plan

I gasped for air, my chest heaving as the weight of the memory finally released its grip on me. My younger self was still there, watching, but the room around us was fading—the edges of the basement blurring as reality began to pull me back.

I staggered, barely able to keep myself upright. My heart was racing; my legs felt weak beneath me, but I had to move. I had to get out. I couldn't stay here; I had to get away from him—away from *me*.

I turned toward the staircase at the far end of the basement, the way out. The old wooden steps stretched before me, seeming impossibly long, but they were my only escape. My breath came in gasps as I forced myself forward, each step echoing through the dimly lit space. I needed to leave this place and never look back.

My legs trembled as I ascended the stairs, each step heavier than the last. The flickering overhead lights cast twisted shadows along the stone walls, and the air grew thicker, as though the sanatorium itself was trying to pull me back down.

I stumbled, nearly falling as I reached for the handrail, my fingers slipping on the cold, rusted metal. The locket around my neck pulsed, a dark energy humming against my chest. No matter how hard I tried, I couldn't tear it off. It felt like a noose tightening around my throat with every step I took away from the basement.

You have to give it more. Evelyn's voice echoed in my mind, sharp and haunting. *Only then will we unlock its true potential.*

I pressed on, ignoring her words, pushing away the memories that clawed at me. The door at the top of the staircase was just ahead—my way out.

I reached the top of the stairs, my legs burning, each step heavier than the last. The door creaked open, revealing the dimly lit corridor stretching toward the front entrance—my escape.

I pushed through the pain, staggering down the hallway. The exit was close now—just ahead. I had only to keep moving. My body protested, but I couldn't stop.

Then, just as I neared the doors, Evelyn stepped out from one of the nearby rooms.

She moved with eerie calm, her back to me at first. For a moment, I thought she hadn't noticed me, but then she turned, her gaze locking onto mine as if she had known I would be here all along.

"Leaving already?" she asked, her voice cold and measured.

I froze, my heart pounding in my chest. "You can't keep me here, Evelyn. I'm done. Done with all of this."

She stepped toward me, her lips curling into a cruel smile. "Done? You think it's that simple?"

I clenched my jaw, stepping back, my hand tightening on the door-frame behind me. "Watch me."

Her eyes narrowed, and her smile faded as she stepped forward. "You don't get to walk away, Harold. This place... the locket... They're a part of you now. You'll never be free from it."

I could feel my pulse racing as she closed the distance between us. I was so close to the exit, but Evelyn stood between me and freedom. Her presence was suffocating, and the weight of her words pressed down on me.

"I don't care," I said, my voice tight. "I'm leaving."

But before I could take another step, something sharp cut through my ankle. I screamed, falling to the ground as pain exploded in my leg. I looked down to see a jagged blade embedded in my flesh, blood pooling around it. My vision blurred from the agony, but I forced myself to move, to crawl away.

Evelyn's voice was colder now, with a dangerous edge to it. "I won't let you leave, Harold. Not until you realize what you are."

I gritted my teeth and tried to pull the blade out, but it was buried deep. Panic surged through me. This wasn't an illusion. It wasn't some hallucination brought on by the locket. It was real, and she was serious.

I looked up, and there she was, standing over me, holding another blade in her hand.

"You've spent your whole life trying to run from this place, from who you really are," she said, her voice low. "But it's time to stop running."

I kicked at her with my good leg, but she grabbed my ankle, yanking me toward her. The pain shot through me like fire. She kneeled, her hand trailing over my injured leg as she examined it.

"You think leaving here will free you?" Her grip tightened. "This is your home, Harold. The locket has bound you to it. You'll never be free."

I gasped for air, trying to push her away, but she was stronger than she looked. She pressed the blade against my leg just enough for me to feel the cold metal on my skin. "You can't run anymore," she whispered.

"Evelyn—" I gasped, my voice trembling with desperation. "You don't have to do this."

Her eyes darkened, an unsettling mix of fury and something far more sinister flickering within them. "This isn't about me, Harold," she said, her voice a low growl. "It's about you. It's always been about you."

Before I could react, she drove the blade straight into my already injured leg.

A searing, white-hot pain tore through me, and I screamed, the sound reverberating through the empty halls. My vision blurred as the agony coursed through my body. She twisted the blade, grinding it into the wound, and my whole leg convulsed with pain.

I thrashed, my hands clawing at the floor, desperate for something— anything—to fight back. My fingers scraped across the cold floor until they found a jagged piece of metal. Gritting my teeth, I swung it blindly, the sharp edge slicing across her arm.

Evelyn let out a guttural yell, her grip slackening as blood dripped from her arm. I seized the opportunity and kicked her with my good leg, sending her stumbling back.

My body screamed in protest as I rolled to the side, somehow forcing myself to my feet. My injured leg felt like it was on fire, blood pouring from the wound, but I couldn't stop. I couldn't stay here.

Evelyn staggered to her feet; her face contorted with fury. "You won't make it out of here," she spat, her voice dripping with venom. "You're already too weak."

Her words dug into me like the blade that had torn through my leg, but I pushed forward, adrenaline overriding the pain, propelling me toward the door. My breath was ragged, each step an agony, but I didn't stop. I could hear her footsteps echoing behind me, but I refused to look back.

"You can't escape what's inside you, Harold," her voice called after me, growing fainter with each step. "No matter where you go, it will follow. It's who you are."

I reached the door—the one that had been stuck before, the one I hadn't been able to open no matter how hard I'd tried. But now, as my trembling hand gripped the handle and pulled, it opened effortlessly, swinging outward as though it had never been locked. For a moment, I stood frozen, surprised that there were no more barriers. No tricks. No more resistance.

Was I really free?

I stepped outside, the cold night air biting at my skin, sharp and unforgiving. The first thing that struck me was how different everything was. The sprawling grounds of the sanatorium were gone. In their place was a vineyard stretching out into the distance, vines swaying gently in the breeze under the pale moonlight.

I glanced back over my shoulder, half-expecting to see the looming structure of the sanatorium behind me. But it wasn't there. The building had vanished as though it had never existed.

My leg buckled beneath me, and I collapsed onto the cold earth, my hands pressing against the wound to slow the bleeding. I gasped, the night air sharp in my lungs. The world spun, and for a moment, all I could hear was my labored breathing.

But then I heard a soft voice, mocking, drifting from somewhere far away.

"You're only running from yourself, Harold," Evelyn's voice echoed in my mind. "And that's a race you'll never win."

I forced myself to sit up, trying to shake off the haze of pain and exhaustion. As I looked around, I noticed something odd. In the vineyard, there was a small shed—weathered, almost out of place amidst the rows of vines.

And standing by it was a figure.

I struggled to my feet, my body screaming in protest with every movement. My injured leg burned, each step sending fresh waves of pain through me, but I limped forward, drawn toward the figure near the shed. As I got closer, I realized who it was.

Ten.

He stood there, watching me with those calm, patient eyes. He said nothing as I approached; he just waited in silence. When I was close enough, I could see the faintest hint of a smile on his lips—almost like he had been expecting me.

I collapsed again, this time at his feet, and he kneeled beside me. Without a word, Ten reached for the locket still hanging from my neck. The moment his fingers brushed the cool metal, something strange happened. Bandages appeared in his hands, along with a small vial of medicine. He worked quickly, wrapping the wound on my leg with steady, precise movements and applying the medicine with care.

The pain dulled just slightly, and I let out a shaky breath.

"Where are Abi and Manny?" I asked, my voice weak but urgent.

Ten paused, his hands stilling for a moment before he answered. "They're gone, Harold. You set them free."

Confusion washed over me. "What do you mean?"

"Harold," Ten said gently, his tone steady and calming. "They were different traits of you. Abi—your abience—represented your avoidance, your tendency to escape from everything that frightens you. And Manny—your mania—was the chaos, the overwhelming emotions that drove you to madness. They weren't separate beings. They were manifestations of your inner struggles that you needed to confront and accept."

My breath hitched as I processed his words, the weight of their meaning settling in. "So, by letting them go... I was finally acknowledging parts of myself."

"Exactly," Ten replied, a soft smile touching his lips. "You've learned to deal with those aspects of who you are. But I'm still here, Harold. Tension. Guilt. Until you face me, you won't find true freedom."

A chill ran down my spine as the realization dawned on me. "Are you saying I still need to face my guilt? The actions I took… the choices I made."

Ten nodded, his expression serious. "Yes. Only by facing that guilt can you let me go. You've faced your fears and your madness, but now you must confront your past. Accept it, and you can truly be free."

I closed my eyes, leaning back against the side of the shed, my mind racing with everything I had to come to terms with. I had accepted the locket and dealt with my madness, but now I realized I still had the darkest parts of myself to face—my guilt and shame.

As I sat there, feeling the cool earth beneath me, a sense of resolve grew within. It was time to confront the past, to reclaim the pieces of myself I had lost along the way. Until I did, I knew I would remain shackled by my own choices.

"I will face it," I murmured, my voice barely above a whisper but filled with newfound determination.

Ten's expression softened, a glimmer of hope in his eyes. "Then you're one step closer, Harold."

CHAPTER 23

A Twist of Fate

The wind rustled through the vineyard, the leaves of the grapevines whispering secrets I wasn't ready to hear. Ten stood beside me, his presence a silent reminder of the burden I carried—the weight of guilt I wasn't sure I could ever put down. I glanced at the locket in my hand, its surface now dull, as if the life it once held had faded. With a deep breath, I threw it away, hurling it into the rows of vines. It disappeared into the greenery, and for a moment, I felt lighter. But it didn't last.

I turned to Ten. "I'll work on it," I said, forcing the words out, more for my benefit than his. "I'll deal with my guilt. I'll face it."

Ten laughed softly, shaking his head. "We both know that's your hardest obstacle, Harold. But sure, tell yourself that."

His laughter echoed in the air, and I felt a cold knot form in my stomach. I couldn't argue with him. Guilt was the one thing I had run from my entire life. It was the reason I had come here, the reason I had gotten trapped in this nightmare. But I had no choice now. I had to confront it.

"Do you think I can ever escape it?" I asked, my voice hardly above a whisper.

Ten's expression shifted, the playful smirk fading as he considered my question. "Escape it? No, that's not possible. But you can learn to coexist with it. Guilt doesn't simply vanish; it becomes a part of who you are. The important thing is not to allow it to take over your life."

I sighed, running my fingers through my hair in exasperation. "That's easier said than done. Just when I believe I've moved on, something drags me back. Like right now." I gestured to the vineyard, feeling the heaviness of the past weighing on me. "This place, this moment—it all brings back memories of what I lost. What I did."

"It's not about what you lost," Ten replied, his tone now serious. "It's about what you still have. You're alive, Harold. You survived the darkness, and now you have the chance to choose a different path. You can't change the past, but you can shape your future."

I gazed at the horizon. "But what if my future is merely a repetition of my past mistakes?"

Ten stepped closer, his gaze piercing. "Then make it a different story. You're the author of your life, Harold. Stop letting the sanatorium dictate your narrative. You have the power to rewrite it."

As I turned my back to Ten and stared at the horizon, I noticed something unsettling. The air rippled, and suddenly, the vineyard seemed to blur at the edges. My heart dropped as I understood what was happening.

I slowly turned back toward where the sanatorium had once stood. And there it was again—looming, ominous, just as it had been before. The run-down building with its decaying façade and crooked windows now stood at the edge of the vineyard as if it had always been there, waiting for me to return.

The cold knot in my stomach tightened. I didn't have to look at Ten to know he was still smirking.

"Looks like your escape didn't last long," he said, his voice dripping with mockery. "Go on, Harold. You know where you belong."

"I don't belong there," I retorted, a flicker of defiance igniting inside me. "I've worked too hard to take back my life. I won't allow it to drag me back in."

Ten raised an eyebrow, his smirk fading slightly. "Then prove it. Face it. You can't ignore your past, but you can confront it. You have a choice now—run back to the comfort of your guilt or step into the unknown and find your strength."

I swallowed the lump in my throat and moved toward the reappeared sanatorium. The gravel crunched under my feet as I approached its front door. My heart pounded with every step, a sense of dread settling over me.

The door creaked as I reached for the handle, a brass relic of another time tarnished by age. I hesitated for a moment, taking a deep breath before pulling it open.

Inside, the air hit me immediately. The same stale, musty scent filled my nose—the smell of decay and forgotten memories. I stepped into the darkened foyer, the warped wooden floor groaning under my weight.

I was back.

A wave of familiarity washed over me as I stood near the front door of the sanatorium. I had thrown away the locket, severing its hold on me.

I glanced around, taking in the dusty interior and the shadows that seemed to whisper memories of my past. I could feel Ten's words replaying in my mind. I had to confront my guilt, not run from it.

With a deep breath, I stepped further into the foyer, the creak of the floorboards beneath me grounding me in the moment. The stale, musty air didn't choke me; it reminded me of the weight I needed to lift. I wouldn't be a prisoner of my past anymore. I was here to reclaim my story. This place, with all its darkness, was merely a backdrop now—a canvas on which I could paint a new beginning.

I approached the front door of the sanatorium, gripping the handle tightly, but it resisted my pull as if determined to keep me locked in.

I glanced around and saw the boarded-up window beside the door. My body acted on instinct. I tore at the boards, ripping them free. The glass behind them shattered as I yanked the last piece of wood away, and without hesitation, I climbed through the broken window.

The jagged edges of the glass sliced at my hands, but I barely felt the pain. All I could think about was getting away. I hit the ground outside, scrambling to my feet and running toward the gate.

My car was still there. I didn't waste a second. I jumped inside, turned the key, and slammed my foot on the gas. The tires screeched as I sped away from the sanatorium, the twisted building disappearing behind me in the rearview mirror.

When I finally reached my apartment, I sat in my car for a moment, trying to catch my breath. My heart was still racing, my hands shaking. But I was out. I had made it home.

I climbed the stairs to my apartment, unlocked the door, and stepped inside. For a moment, relief washed over me. The familiar surroundings—the scattered books, the messy bed, the worn-out couch—all felt like a refuge.

But then I saw it.

I stood there, frozen, staring at the table. The smell of the cooked food lingered faintly in the air. The chicken croquettes, perfectly arranged, sat untouched. Everything should have been normal. But it wasn't.

The eerie stillness of the scene made my skin crawl. My heart began to race, the weight of the moment pressing down on me. Something was wrong. Something was very wrong.

I shook my head, trying to shake off the unease. I was exhausted—physically and mentally drained from everything that had happened. Without another glance at the table, I made my way to the bedroom, my body feeling heavier with each step.

I collapsed onto the bed, sinking into the sheets. The familiar scent of home enveloped me, but it offered no comfort. My mind was racing, a jumbled mess of thoughts I couldn't untangle. The sanatorium, the vineyard, Ten's mocking laughter—they all bled together in a nightmare I couldn't escape.

Eventually, sleep came, pulling me under.

I jolted awake, my heart pounding as if I had been running. For a moment, I lay there, disoriented. The room was silent except for the faint rustling of the curtains in the breeze. My hands clenched into fists as I tried to calm myself. That's when I felt something cold and familiar in my hand.

Confusion flooded my mind. Slowly, I raised my hand and looked down.

The locket.

I stared at it, my heart skipping a beat. No. This wasn't possible. I had thrown it away. I had left it behind at the vineyard. But here it was, cold and heavy in my palm. Panic rose in my chest. How? How was it back?

I sat up, turning the locket over in my hands. The details were perfect—too perfect. Then it hit me. This wasn't the same locket. It was a replica, down to the finest detail, but something about it felt... off.

A sickening dread settled in the pit of my stomach. I glanced around the room, my eyes darting from the door to the window. The questions started piling up, sucking me. Had I ever really left the sanatorium? Was any of this real?

Suddenly, I heard a faint creak, followed by soft footsteps. My eyes snapped to the doorway, and there she was.

Emily.

She stood there, smiling at me as if everything were fine. Her presence sent a chill down my spine, yet she looked perfectly normal, almost... happy. "Good morning," she said softly, her voice carrying a warmth that felt all too wrong.

I blinked, trying to process the sight of her standing there and the casualness of her greeting. Morning? I turned to the window, my heart racing. Sunlight streamed in through the curtains, casting a soft glow across the room.

"Emily?" I whispered, my voice barely audible, laced with confusion. "What's happening?"

She tilted her head, a bemused expression crossing her face. "What do you mean? Everything's okay." She approached me with a nonchalant air as if the events of the past few days had never happened.

I stared at her, struggling to make sense of it all. Was it possible that everything that had happened—the sanatorium, Ten, the nightmare —had been a dream? No. No, I couldn't believe that. I *knew* it was real. It had to be real.

But the morning light, Emily's serene demeanor—it all felt like a cruel joke, a mockery of my sanity.

As she stood beside me, placing a hand on my shoulder, I fought the urge to recoil. My mind was racing. I couldn't tell if I was still trapped in some elaborate illusion or if something even worse was at play.

The more I thought about it, the more the lines between reality and illusion began to blur. How much of what I had experienced could I trust? Was I still fighting something evil? Or had I been a victim of a larger game I didn't fully understand?

I glanced at the locket in my hand again, the replica now feeling heavier, more ominous. A cold realization crept over me—maybe none of this had been real. Maybe I had been the architect of my suffering all along.

Emily's voice snapped me back to the moment. "Why don't you get ready for breakfast? I made your favorite—blueberry pancakes and an omelet."

I blinked, staring at her. Her calm, cheerful demeanor was so wrong. Everything about this was wrong. But she stood there, waiting, her expression so sincere it made me question everything.

As I nodded numbly, she turned to leave. I heard her say something under her breath, something about her dissertation. The words were indistinct, but it was enough to set off a distant alarm in my mind.

It was too normal, too casual, as if none of this had ever happened.

The feeling gnawed at me as I watched her walk away, her demeanor unshaken, like the past had been erased. What did she just say? A knot tightened in my chest, but the clarity slipped away as I stumbled toward the bathroom in a daze. The water from the shower felt like a lifeline, grounding me in something physical, something real.

But the questions never stopped.

Had it all been a dream? A figment of my imagination?

When I finished, I dressed and walked back out, finding Emily seated at the table, just as she had promised, with a plate of blueberry pancakes and a fluffy omelet waiting for me. She smiled as I sat down, her eyes full of warmth. She said nothing, just quietly placing a fork in front of me, watching as I hesitated.

The food smelled delicious—the kind of breakfast she used to make when everything was *right*.

She didn't speak. She just smiled.

I picked up the fork, my mind still spinning, and slowly took a bite. It tasted perfect, exactly the way I remembered. But deep down, I knew—it wasn't.

Something was still very wrong.

But neither of us said a word.

CHAPTER 24

Letting Go of Emily

The pancakes were perfect—just like she used to make them. Fluffy, golden, and rich with the smell of blueberries, each bite bringing with it the echo of a simpler time. A time when everything made sense. But the comfort I should've felt only deepened the pit in my stomach. Every forkful felt wrong as if the food itself was part of the lie.

Emily sat across from me, her eyes soft and affectionate, her smile warm and reassuring. "Go on, Harold," she said gently. "There's no rush—we've got all the time in the world."

Her voice was exactly as I remembered—sweet, gentle, reassuring. But it didn't sit right. The way she looked at me, the way her smile never quite reached her eyes—it all felt hollow—a carefully constructed façade.

I put my fork down, the metal clinking against the plate louder than it should have been. The weight of the food sat heavy in my stomach. "Emily..." My voice was hoarse. "Stop pretending."

Her smile flickered just for a second before she regained her composure. "I don't know what you're talking about," she said smoothly. "This is real, Harold. This is us." She leaned in slightly, her tone softening. "Don't you see? We can be happy again, just like we were before all of this happened."

"No," I said, shaking my head, trying to keep my thoughts straight. "You're not... you're not who you used to be. I know what you're doing."

Her eyes darkened, a cold glint flashing behind the false tenderness she tried to maintain. "What am I doing, Harold?" she asked, her voice dripping with mocking curiosity. "Tell me." She leaned back in her chair, crossing her arms as if daring me to speak.

I stood, the chair scraping against the floor as I pushed back from the table. The air felt thick, suffocating, as if the room itself were closing in on me. "You're not who I fell in love with," I said, my voice barely a whisper. "I see it now... The real you."

She didn't flinch. Instead, she laughed—a soft, hollow sound that sent a chill down my spine. "You always were so dramatic," she said, her eyes locking onto mine, her smile now devoid of any warmth. "You're confused, Harold. You've been through so much. But you don't have to fight anymore. Just stay with me. We can have everything you've always wanted."

Her words dug into me like a blade, each carefully chosen to twist the guilt, the longing, and the love I still held for the woman she used to be. But I couldn't ignore the truth anymore. "I know who you are, Emily," I said, the words catching in my throat. "And I know this isn't real."

Her smile faltered, the mask slipping. "Real?" she repeated, her voice low, dangerous. "This is as real as it gets, Harold. You're here. I'm here. Why can't you just accept that?" Her tone grew sharper, more insistent. "You want this. You've always wanted this. Us. Together."

I shook my head, my vision starting to blur as dizziness washed over me. "What... did you do?" My voice was unsteady, my grip tightening on the edge of the table as the room began to spin. The walls seemed to warp and bend, everything blurring around me.

She stood up slowly, her expression hardening as she watched me struggle. "You never could let things go, could you?" she said, her voice soft but laced with contempt. "Always fighting. Always pushing. But it's over now, Harold. This is your new reality." She stepped toward me, her eyes gleaming with triumph. "And you can't do a thing about it."

I tried to move, to speak, but my body felt like it was sinking, my limbs heavy, my thoughts unraveling. I collapsed to the floor, my head spinning, the edges of my vision going dark. Her figure loomed over me, her smile cold and triumphant. The last thing I saw before everything went black was her standing there, watching me fall.

When I woke, the world was cold and sterile. My head throbbed, and the faint buzzing in my ears made it hard to focus. The walls around me were stark white—padded, like the kind you'd see in asylums. There was no door, no window. Just a bed and four blank walls that felt like they were closing in.

I got up, my heart racing. "What the hell is this?"

Then, the door clicked open. Emily stepped inside, smiling that same familiar smile—warm, too warm for the cold emptiness around us.

"Good morning, Harold," she said with unsettling cheer. "Welcome home."

"Home?" I struggled to stand, my muscles quivering in bewilderment. "What is this? Where are we?"

"This is where you belong now," she said softly, moving closer. "Where you've always belonged. You've been running for too long, but now... you're exactly where I need you to be."

Her words hit like a hammer to my chest. I stepped back, barely able to breathe. "You don't need me, Emily. You used to... protect me. You always cared about me. What happened to you?"

Her smile faded, replaced by something darker—colder. "I still care, Harold. But not in the way you think. What I care about is my mother's vision. And you're part of it. Everything I've done has been to serve her, and that's all that matters."

"Your mother's vision?" My voice cracked. "You used to watch over me—protect me. Where's that, Emily? Does she not care about me at all anymore?"

For a moment, I saw something flicker in her eyes—a shadow of the woman I remembered. But then it vanished, replaced with the unyielding loyalty she'd always had for Evelyn. "It's not about love or family anymore, Harold. What we were as kids... It doesn't matter now. What matters is the plan. The plan I've followed my whole life, the one that will change everything."

I clenched my fists, my chest tightening. She was gone—lost to whatever brainwashing Evelyn had ingrained in her. I wanted to fight for her; to believe I could still save her. But deep down, I knew the truth.

It wasn't Emily that had held me prisoner. It was my guilt. My need to save her—to fix what I thought was broken. But I was the one dragging us both down.

I swallowed hard, feeling the weight of years pressing down on me. "You're wrong," I whispered, stepping forward, my voice stronger now. "I'm not your pawn anymore. I won't be part of your mother's sick game. You believe you have control over me, but you don't."

Her smile faltered, confusion creeping into her eyes. "Harold—"

"No," I cut her off, voice firm. "I'm done carrying the blame. Done trying to fix what you and Evelyn twisted. I may not remember everything I did, but I know enough. I was manipulated. Used. And now... I'm letting you go."

Her eyes flashed with anger, but there was something else too—doubt. For the first time, she didn't seem so sure of herself.

"You don't understand," she said, her voice sharp. "You need us. You need me. You think you can just walk away from this?"

"Yes," I said quietly, stepping closer. "I can. I have to."

The air between us felt heavy, her fury manifesting in the trembling walls around me. And as the tension hung thick, another presence emerged from the doorway—Ten.

"Harold," Ten's voice was faint, like a whisper carried by the wind. "You've done it. You've faced the truth."

Emily turned toward him, her eyes wide with panic, her calm veneer shattered. "No," she growled, her voice laced with desperation. "You don't get to take him from me. Not now. Not after everything!"

Her words were wild and feral, as though something inside her was unraveling. She lunged toward me, her hands trembling, reaching as if trying to reclaim the control that had slipped from her grasp.

But Ten stepped forward, his form flickering, fragile as if the very act of staying at this moment was pulling him apart. His eyes met mine, soft but full of understanding. "Harold," he said, his voice quieter now, gentler, "I can't stay. You've freed yourself... from her. From all of it."

Emily's expression contorted into a frightening blend of rage and shock. "No!" she shrieked, her voice breaking with rage. "You're mine! You were always mine!"

Her hands reached out, clawing at the air between us, but Ten moved faster, his fading form still strong enough to grab her arm. Emily fought against him, her struggle wild and frantic, her eyes locking with mine as if begging for something—control, power, a hold she would never have again.

"Thank you," Ten whispered; his grip on her was unyielding. His eyes held something I never expected to see—gratitude. "This is my end. And it's your beginning."

Emily screamed again, her voice piercing the air, filled with all the years of manipulation and control she'd wielded. Her fury was palpable, and for a moment, her gaze softened, not in love but in the realization that she had lost. She was losing everything.

Ten's body flickered one final time, and in a blinding flash of light, both of them—Emily and Ten—disappeared, swallowed by the brilliance, leaving behind only silence.

The room was still. Empty.

I stood there, frozen, my chest heaving with the weight of what had happened. The weight that had clung to me for so long—Emily's control, the guilt, the endless chase—was gone. The air felt lighter and clearer, but it didn't feel like victory.

Emily was gone. Ten was gone.

I was free.

I sank to the floor, my legs giving out beneath me, the emptiness settling in. The relief was there, yes, but so was the hollow ache of loss. Not for Emily—not for who she had become—but for the lover I once knew, the one who was lost long before this moment.

I had freed myself, but in the process, I had lost everything I thought I was fighting for.

And now, for the first time in a long time... I had to confront the truth of my existence without them.

CHAPTER 25

A New Beginning

I stumbled out of the padded room, the door ajar, beckoning me into the light. I expected the cold air and the familiar discomfort of stepping back into the sanatorium's hallways. But something felt off. The hallway ahead of me seemed too bright, too... clean, as if it had been waiting for me. It was quiet, unnervingly so, and with each step, my unease deepened.

When I reached the front entrance, there was the locket glimmering from the door handle. It was out of place. Why would it be here again? My heart sank. *Hadn't I thrown this thing away?* My fingers twitched, a feeling of dread creeping up my spine.

I glanced at the window; the same one I had broken through before. Without a second thought, I climbed through it, landing in the soft grass outside. But as I took a breath of fresh air, my chest tightened. The sky was the same muted gray, the trees frozen in their stillness as if the world itself hadn't moved since I last escaped.

I looked back at the sanatorium, its looming structure casting a familiar shadow over me. The car that had been parked in front, the one where I found Emily's journal—it wasn't there. My car lay in ruins against the gate, exactly where it had crashed when I first arrived. A creeping realization set in.

"No..." I whispered, shaking my head. "This can't be right."

I looked down at the locket in my hand, its surface cold and unyielding. The weight of it seemed heavier than ever, as if it were tethering me to something I couldn't escape. *I thought I got rid of it. I thought it was over.* But here it was again, clinging to me.

A strange thought crept into my mind, unsettling and sharp. *What if I never left?*

The world around me blurred slightly as if the edges of my vision were softening. *Emily.* What if she wasn't real? What if none of it was?

I could still remember her smile, her voice, and the way she held my hand. But the details... They felt distant now, out of focus, slipping through my mind like sand through my fingers. *What if she was never there at all?*

My thoughts spiraled faster. What if the sanatorium, the escape, everything—*none of it was real?*

The realization hit me like a cold wave, knocking the breath from my lungs. I hadn't escaped anything. I was still here—still trapped.

Suddenly, I found myself back inside the padded room. I staggered, gripping the locket tighter. The world I thought I had escaped was nothing but a lie—a carefully crafted illusion designed to keep me running in circles.

My hands shook, and my chest tightened as I stared at the locket. "I'm still in the sanatorium," I muttered, my voice barely a whisper. The truth crushed me. *Everything I thought I had been fighting for, all of it —just a fantasy.*

But then something shifted.

I squeezed my eyes shut, focusing on the pounding of my heart and the sound of my breath. *What if I could fight back?* What if this reality wasn't as unbreakable as it seemed? I wasn't just a victim in this prison. *I had built it, too.*

The locket had twisted my mind, fed me lies, and warped my sense of what was real. But *I* had the power to break it. I had built this world, and now I would tear it down.

The realization didn't crush me—it *freed* me.

I stared at the locket, now resting calmly in my palm. It no longer glimmered ominously; it felt cold and lifeless. The truth washed over me like ice water: the locket had fed off my mind, my fears, and my guilt. It had twisted me into the leader of the darkness that consumed me, trapping me in my own prison. But I saw through the illusion now. I had the power to end this.

I clenched my jaw and took a deep breath, grounding myself in the reality that lay before me. "It's not real," I said firmly. "None of this is real."

With that acknowledgment, the sanatorium around me began to warp, the padded walls flickering like a broken film. I felt the locket's energy intensify, the familiar grip tightening around my chest as it fought to maintain its hold. But I refused to let it ensnare me again.

"Enough!" I shouted, rising to my feet, a surge of defiance coursing through me. *This place was never my home. This was never my life.* I felt the heat of anger burn through the haze of despair. It was time to confront the heart of this darkness and take back my life.

As the walls began to dissolve, I focused on the locket, envisioning it as the source of all my pain. "You want to keep me here? You think you can control me? Watch me take it all back." I held it high, feeling its cold metal press against my palm, an anchor tethered to my past.

But this time, I wouldn't let fear win. I surged forward, throwing the locket against the wall. It hit with a resounding crack, sending shards of darkness spiraling through the air. The locket's power faltered, and I could feel the grip of the sanatorium begin to loosen.

"I'm done with this shit!" I yelled, grabbing a nearby chair and smashing it against the locket, feeling a wild exhilaration take over as I destroyed the object of my torment. The walls trembled, the ground shook, and the air crackled with energy. *I would end this once and for all.*

But I wasn't done yet. I could still feel the remnants of the sanatorium pulling at me, desperate to keep me trapped. I needed to burn it all away.

I glanced around the room, searching for a way to set this place ablaze. I stumbled toward the door, determined to escape this cell. As I threw open the door, the corridor beyond stretched out, dimly lit and echoing with whispers of my past.

I dashed down the hall, my pulse quickening with each step. Finally, I spotted a laboratory door slightly ajar. I rushed inside, scanning the room filled with various chemicals and equipment. My eyes landed on a container labeled "Cyclohexane."

I grabbed it without hesitation, its weight reassuring in my hands. This would do the trick.

As I turned to leave, my fingers brushed against a small pack in my pants pocket. Matches! I had forgotten they were there.

Returning to the padded room, I poured the contents of the container over the remnants of the locket and the walls that had confined me for too long. The strong, pungent smell filled the air.

"FUCK YOU!" I yelled, striking a match and holding the flame above the soaked surface. "This ends now!"

The fire leaped eagerly, consuming the remnants of the locket first. I watched in awe as the flames danced and roared to life, engulfing the twisted memories that had bound me. Heat radiated from the blaze, and each flicker was a cleansing burn that fueled my resolve. The shadows it cast began to dissipate, swirling away like memories turned to ash.

I stepped back as the flames spread, racing along the walls like a living creature, eager to devour everything in its path. Panic ignited within me, not from fear but from exhilaration. I had lit the spark that would free me, but I needed to escape before the inferno consumed all.

My heart raced as I dashed for the door, the heat intensifying with each passing moment. The padded room was already lost, the air thickening with smoke as I sprinted down the corridor, the flames licking hungrily at my heels. I burst through the broken window and into the night, the cold air hitting my face like a splash of icy water.

My car was waiting for me. I leaped inside, my fingers fumbling as I struggled to start the engine. I glanced back at the sanatorium, its structure illuminated by the roaring fire, each window glowing like a hollow eye watching its own demise. For the first time, I felt the pull of the locket weaken, its sinister grip loosening as the flames engulfed the sanatorium.

With a deep breath, I finally got the engine running; the sound of it was a triumphant roar over the crackling inferno. I stole one last look at the building as it began to buckle, the flames consuming it from within. I felt a surge of freedom flood my veins—a smile broke across my face.

As the sanatorium crumbled, I could almost hear the locket's defeated whisper, its power dissipating into the night like smoke. I gripped the steering wheel, laughter bubbling up from within me, a joyful release as I drove away from the ashes of my torment. The past had been laid to rest, and now I was alive—truly alive.

Arriving home, I stumbled through the front door, the familiar surroundings a stark contrast to the chaos I had just escaped. The silence enveloped me, almost soothing in its embrace. I made my way to the bathroom, the mirror reflecting my weary face.

I turned on the shower, letting the hot water cascade over me, washing away the remnants of fear. I glanced down at the nasty wound on my leg and ankle, raw and angry. Grabbing a clean cloth, I gently cleaned the gash, wincing at the sting, but I welcomed the discomfort as a reminder of my fight. With each dab of antiseptic, I felt more grounded, more real.

Afterward, I made my way into the kitchen, grabbing a cold beer from the fridge. The chill against my palm offered a brief comfort as I sank onto the couch and took a long sip, letting the bitter taste anchor me. With my eyes closed, I savored a rare moment of quiet, feeling, for once, that the chaos had loosened its grip.

But then, a deep, rhythmic thump broke the silence—a sound like a heartbeat. My eyes flew open, and my eyes fixed on the locket lying on the table, intact. My pulse quickened as I picked it up, the metal cool and disturbingly solid beneath my fingers.

In an instant, my familiar surroundings faded away. I stood in a vast, dimly lit hall where the sharp scent of antiseptic mingled with something ritualistic. The walls of the sanatorium stretched around me, though altered as if pulled from the deepest recesses of my mind.

A crowd filled the hall, each face a fractured piece of myself. Manny grinned nearby, his eyes glinting with unsettling humor. Ten stood off to the side, his gaze cold and analytical, observing with a detachedness that felt foreign yet familiar. Abi, his young face tinged with both innocence and sorrow, looked at me with an understanding far beyond his years.

Others hovered in the shadows—strangers yet somehow familiar, fragments of paths I hadn't taken or versions of myself I hadn't met. They encircled a dark altar at the room's center, each moving in a silent, rhythmic ritual.

At the edge of the crowd stood Emily, her gaze piercing as she lifted the locket. She tilted her head, gesturing for me to approach. The crowd parted, opening a path toward the altar. Each step brought me closer, the heartbeat echoing louder, its rhythm pulsing through me.

The ritual around me grew more intense, each figure moving in unison, expressions frozen in a trance that mirrored my turmoil.

As I neared the altar, a hollow realization sank in: This wasn't freedom; it was a trap. The locket wasn't an escape but an anchor, chaining me to this shadowed world within the sanatorium walls. I looked down at the altar, the heartbeat now a deafening pulse. Emily's smirk was the last thing I saw before I stepped into the circle, my fate sealed.

The rhythm slowed, and I joined the ritual, bound to this endless labyrinth—a prisoner in the darkest corners of my mind.

The Lyaeus Sanatorium

The image depicts the ominous Lyaeus Sanatorium, with its labyrinthine corridors and shadowy rooms encircling a tranquil courtyard. At its center stands the tower where Dr. Harold Morgan uncovers mysteries tied to Emily's disappearance and the dark locket's sinister legacy.

The Unmasked Villain by Chris Witt is a gripping mystery thriller that takes readers on a suspenseful journey through dark secrets and unexpected twists. With compelling characters and edge-of-your-seat

tension, it's a must-read for fans of crime and intrigue.

A Memory's Web: A Conspiracy Unveiled

" This writer takes you beyond your curiosity and into the story itself. The storyline is intense and keeps the reader intrigued from beginning to end. A must read! "

-- Laurie NYC

"A Memory's Web: A Conspiracy Unveiled" by Chris Witt is a gripping psychological thriller that plunges readers into a maze of forgotten pasts and chilling conspiracies. Witt keeps the suspense high, delivering twist after twist as the protagonist fights to uncover buried truths.

This dark and compelling mystery challenges perceptions and keeps readers on the edge of their seats. Perfect for fans of suspenseful, mind-bending thrillers, "A Memory's Web" will linger with you long after the final page"

Connect with the Author

Email: Info@chriswittpublishing.com

Follow me on Twitter: https://x.com/ChrisWitt478348

Follow me on Facebook:https://www.facebook.com/profile.php?id=61561870475800

Follow me on Instagram: https://www.instagram.com/chriswitt467/

Website: https://booksbychriswitt.com/

TikTok:

https://www.tiktok.com/@chriswittauthor?_t=ZT-8tr8ymDAze6&_r=1

Chris Witt is an emerging voice in contemporary literature, captivating readers with his evocative storytelling and deep emotional insight. With a background in creative writing and a passion for exploring the human condition. Born and raised in a small town, Chris developed a love for books at an early age, spending countless hours immersed in the works of classic and contemporary authors.

Chris's debut novel, "A Memory's Web ," quickly garnered critical acclaim, establishing him as a fresh and innovative voice in fiction.

In addition to his novels, Chris has also penned several short stories and essays. His works often explore themes of identity, memory, and the human condition, resonating deeply with readers across the globe. Chris Witt currently resides in a quiet small town home, where he is hard at work on his next novel. His dedication to his craft and his ability to touch the hearts and minds of his readers ensure that his stories will be cherished for years to come.